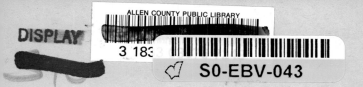

Dear Readers,

This spring, we're willing to bet a *woman's* fancy will turn to love—with four brand-new Bouquet romances full of passion and laughter.

Award-winning author Vivian Leiber begins a three-book series titled "The Men of Sugar Mountain" with **One Touch,** as high school sweethearts confront the past—and dream of a shared future. Beloved Silhouette and Zebra author Suzanne McMinn offers **It Only Takes a Moment,** a charming present-day fairy tale in which a feisty woman proves that even a prince must remember he's a man.

Nothing stays the same forever. In **Charmed and Dangerous,** Silhouette author Lynda Simmons presents a woman who never thought her childhood buddy would ever offer anything more than a shoulder to lean on—until she discovers he's willing to give so much more. Last is Anna DeForest's **The Cowboy and the Heiress,** the passionate tale of a woman searching for independence and finding that true love is the greatest freedom of all.

With spring flowers ready to bloom, what could be more fitting than a Bouquet of four fabulous romances from us to you?

Kate Duffy
Editorial Director

ROMANCE

ONE KISS

The car doors slammed in unison. TJ stood on one side of the big Mustang, Paige on the other.

"Whoa," TJ exclaimed, rubbing his jaw.

"Mistake," Paige said firmly, planting her palms on the edge of the door.

"You think so?"

She nodded vigorously. "Absolutely a mistake."

"I don't know. Actually, it felt pretty—"

"Don't say it. It's too late for this."

"For what?"

"For a relationship."

"We already have a relationship. We've had one for years. That there thing in the car was a *kiss.*"

They both looked at the backseat as if it were Cupid with an inch-thick rap sheet and hundreds of outstanding arrest warrants.

TJ squared his shoulders. He had put his weight on his hands, balancing on the side of the car. But now that he knew what he wanted and knew it was right, he straightened. "I want you, Paige. And I think—no, I know—you want me, too. Your lips don't lie."

She moaned, shaking her head. "I made love to you once and I wanted to believe I could put that night in a box and close the lid tight." Her voice cracked. "But it changed my life."

He hated the distance between them, the metal and leather interior and inches that stretched into feet. If he had her in his arms, he could overcome any objections. Another kiss was all it would take. One touch—and she'd be his . . . .

THE MEN
OF SUGAR MOUNTAIN:
ONE TOUCH

VIVIAN LEIBER

Zebra Books
Kensington Publishing Corp.

http://www.zebrabooks.com

ZEBRA BOOKS are published by

Kensington Publishing Corp.
850 Third Avenue
New York, NY 10022

First Printing: April, 2000
10 9 8 7 6 5 4 3 2 1

Printed in the United States of America

PROLOGUE

The woman in the red suit wore a name tag identifying her as:

> HI, MY NAME IS JANET.
> HOW MAY I HELP YOU?

She was just about out of patience.

"I can only put one person's name on the birth certificate in the space for a mother. Got it? So pick one. Preferably the name of the woman who has given birth to the child in question. I'll take any name. Just pick one."

She spun her chair toward the computer screen, her fingers poised above the keypad.

Paige Burleson, Kate Henderson, and Zoe Kinnear leaned over the counter, trying to get a peek at the woman's computer screen. The space allowed for the mother's name looked unbearably small, nearly stingy.

"But we want all our names on the birth certificate," Zoe said. "We agreed. We all count as this child's mother. We've been through so much together.

And we all want to take responsibility for him. We love him."

"Put my name. Everyone's going to think it's me anyhow," Kate said, flipping her long blond curls behind her shoulder. "They'll just say sin runs in the family."

Janet glanced at the clock. Almost noon. County workers were given exactly thirty minutes for lunch and she didn't want to lose one precious second dealing with this trio.

"My parents would die," Paige said, "but since I'm never getting married this might be their only chance to have a grandchild."

"You're young, girl. You don't know whether you'll marry or not," Janet cautioned, feeling unaccountably drawn to advise the slim brunette. "The right man could come along any moment."

"He already has," Paige said.

"Stop moping and tell him that making love wasn't simply comforting him after Jack's death. It was the culmination of your entire relationship," Zoe advised.

"Sure, and he'd listen," Kate said.

"I know I'm never marrying," Paige insisted. "So this baby is all I've got. And I want to be part of a family with my two girlfriends. Put me down."

"I won't allow you to put your name on the birth certificate without mine," Zoe said. "We agreed."

Janet eased open the lowest drawer of her desk and pulled out her lunch bag. This wasn't as bad as the time the woman insisted Baltar from the planet Gorgon be listed as the father of her baby. Or the time a couple from somewhere not around here repeated their baby's name again and again—a seventeen-syllable word punctuated with odd clicks and hisses that couldn't be reduced to simple phonetics. Janet had typed the name Sam into the computer and wished whatever school district that got that kid five years hence good luck.

"Ladies," she broke in as Kate and Zoe insisted that all three of them should be listed. "You have got to choose one of you to be the mom. I'll help you out here. Which one of you gave birth to the baby?"

"Me," Kate said. "I should be the one."

"I didn't ask who it should be," Janet snapped. "I asked who it was. I'll make it simple on you. Which one of you got morning sickness?"

"I guess you were always feeling hideous in the morning," Paige said to Zoe.

"You were the one with cravings," Zoe replied.

Janet stared heavenward for guidance.

"Ladies, which one of you went to the hospital with labor pains?"

"None of us," Paige said. "We've spent the summer at my parents' cottage, just the three of us, waiting for our little arrival. We didn't get to the hospital in time."

Janet muttered a weary invective. She typed the name Paige Kate Zoe into the space for the mother's name.

"Child's full name."

"Teddy," Zoe said. "We like the name Teddy. For the president. The first Roosevelt president."

Janet shrugged. They could name the child Millard P. Fillmore for all she cared.

"Last name."

The girls looked momentarily confused.

"There isn't going to be one," Zoe said.

Janet raised a finger.

"Now, ladies. You have had your fun, but a birth certificate is a very important document. Stop playing with me."

That finger, which was shoved into each of their faces in turn, produced its intended effect.

"No, ma'am," Zoe said, her apple-green eyes opened wide. "I mean, yes, ma'am."

"Absolutely not playing with you," Paige said, shaking her head. "Ma'am."

"Not at all," Kate cried.

"How old are you?" Janet asked.

"Eighteen," Paige said.

"Eighteen," Zoe said.

"Seventeen," Kate said.

"Too young to be mothers. I oughta call Children and Family Services down here and—"

"Last name Sugar Mountain," Kate erupted.

"What kind of—" Janet demanded.

"Sugar is the middle name," Kate said. Her friends nodded. "Mountain's the last name. Please don't call Children and Family Services. They came out to my house once and wanted to put me in a foster home. Please, ma'am, don't call them. They'll just make trouble for us."

Her naked fear roused Janet's sympathy.

"I guess you're right. Sometimes they go a little overboard. All right, Teddy Sugar Mountain," she typed. She sat back on her chair, from which she had scarcely noticed rising. "Now, do you wish to list a father?"

"Is it going to be another problem if we don't?" Zoe asked.

"It's the only thing you ladies have done this morning that isn't going to be a problem," Janet said. "Half the certificates I do these days don't list one. Not like when I started here. Nosirreebob! When I got this desk, all babies had fathers—and all babies had only one mother!"

A tiny hiccup and mewing sounded at Zoe's feet. She picked Teddy up out of his carrier and jiggled him in her arms. Janet, who had seen a procession of babies—small, big, thin, fat, beautiful, ugly, yowling, red faced, rheumy eyed, yawning, wheezing or drooling—grudgingly admitted that Teddy was cuter than most, bigger than average, milder mannered than many. In fact, Teddy Sugar Mountain was imbued with such a peaceful countenance, unaided by pacifier or bottle, that Janet allowed as how these three mothers just might be all right.

"Taking him in for his two-week checkup, are you?" she asked gruffly.

"Right after we finish up here," Zoe assured her.

"Maybe we should list the father as Skylar," Paige said. "We all have a piece of our heart that we've lost to a Skylar."

Janet tore her gaze from the mesmerizing baby.

"And just what is a Skylar?" she asked.

"There are three Skylar brothers," Kate said.

"I'm not going to list three fathers on that computer."

"That's okay," Paige said. "There used to be four brothers. TJ, Matt, Win, and Jack. Handsome as men could be. Then there was an accident on the mountain. A safety line that broke. TJ held on to the line, on to Jack, while the other two, Win and Matt, ran for help."

"Really?" Janet said, opening her lunch bag. She felt oddly limp and as wrung out as a washcloth. It was noon. Thirty minutes before the next certificate needed to be printed. "Want a sandwich?"

"Oh, no, thanks, but go right ahead," Paige said. "You see, I loved—well, I admit it—still love TJ. But he thinks of me as a little sister. Or a pal."

"Mm-hmm," Janet murmured, biting down on bologna and cheese with mustard. "Go ahead. What about the accident?"

"Maybe I should start at the beginning. We grew up on Sugar Mountain. The little town, just sixty miles west of here. All six of us."

Janet swallowed.

"Seven," she corrected. "Four brothers, three of you."

"You're right," Paige said, "and the Skylar brothers were like the princes of a beautiful kingdom. Then one day . . ."

ONE

Paige put the past several years into a box her secretary Nelly brought up from the mail room.

There wasn't much.

A crystal paperweight with the logo of an athletic shoe company that had gone public—every lawyer who worked on filing the necessary documents with the Securities and Exchange Commission had been presented with one. There were the three sterling silver bowls commemorating when she broke, rebroke, and rebroke again the firm's record of client-billable hours in a year—she used one for paper clips, the second for rubber bands, and the third for jelly beans. There was a Ming dynasty vase brought back from China by a wealthy and decidedly grateful financier who had used Paige to negotiate entry into the Chinese marketplace.

In the box Paige also put her passport, her pension statement, her severance paycheck, and the coffee mug from TJ's Wall Street company.

On the windowsill was an aloe plant neglected so long and so badly that Paige thought it was dead. She decided to leave it where it was for the next lawyer to take this office space.

And of course, there was a photograph that was her treasure and a reproach. She had put the rest of the framed pictures in the box—Zoe holding baby Teddy on the porch of her white Cape Cod house, Kate's wedding picture, Teddy dressed up as Peter Cottontail for the Sugar Mountain Elementary School Spring Sing. But there was one photograph that she couldn't bring herself to touch. Not yet.

So all that remained on her desk was a white coffee ring and a photograph of her and TJ.

Paige had seldom seen the expensive rosewood finish in the years since she had joined the firm of Greenough, Challenger & Redmond. Up until this morning, it had been covered with papers—court documents, correspondence from clients, angry letters from opposing counsel, Xeroxed statutes, firm memos—so much paper that a pale, busy glow had seemed always to emanate from the surface of her desk. At the very bottom of the paper mountain Paige had found a memo upon which her secretary Nelly had tacked an urgent Post-it note. The memo urged attorneys to R.S.V.P. for the Christmas party.

Christmas 1998.

With the desk cleared and the drawers emptied, Paige took a deep breath and picked up the silver-framed picture.

Her hair was longer then—ten years ago the words *professional* or *office appropriate* weren't part of her vocabulary or her grooming habits. In the picture, a single braid snaked down her back, with sun-bleached tendrils crowding her face. Now she wore a sleek bob that never, ever disobeyed.

And when was the last time she had worn hiking

boots and jeans? Those favorites—easy to wear, washable. Now she wore gray suits, navy blue suits, black suits, pinstriped suits, suits for mergers, suits for acquisitions, suits for days she'd spend in court, only slightly less severe suits for days she'd be in the office. And paired with these were silk blouses that were meant to feminize her appearance, but that, in truth, made her all the more daunting.

Even now, on her last day in the stuffy atmosphere of a top-drawer law firm, she wore a pale ivory silk blouse buttoned within an inch of her face, a gray wool crepe suit cut with severe precision to the middle of her knee, and black pumps that gave her two inches in height.

Seen in this picture taken on the Sugar Mountain slopes just two days before the tragedy, TJ was frequently assumed by clients and visiting attorneys to be a husband—or, using modern, cautious language, her "significant other." There was no mistaking the adoring gaze of her younger self for that of a younger sister or casual acquaintance. No, this was a picture of a woman in love. And a man who was worth it. Big shouldered, square jawed, dark hair streaked with blond that didn't come from a box at the drugstore or a Park Avenue salon but was the blessing of the sun at high altitudes.

A few months ago, an attorney who had been ushered into her office for a late-night negotiating session had taken a long look at the pictures composed on her desk and commented that TJ looked like a real powerhouse of a man.

"Not that a woman can't be a powerhouse," he'd quickly added.

Paige had let the comment pass, knowing that men often felt off balance around her. Why? She had no clue, except perhaps that hard work and no-nonsense diligence from a woman could be mistaken for ball busting.

"He looks familiar," the attorney had continued. "Does he work on the Street?"

Meaning, of course, Wall Street. The only street that mattered to some New Yorkers.

"It's TJ Skylar."

"Really?" Impressed. Very.

"He's a friend."

The word *friend* had elicited a soft mew of sympathy that she found annoying. But she did not correct the apparent impression that she was a discarded girlfriend or a soon-to-be-discarded girlfriend or a soon-to-tire-of-TJ's-renowned-antipathy-to-marriage girlfriend.

Instead, Paige had turned her annoyance inward, and by doing so, she'd extracted even more concessions on behalf of her client. She was a professional that way.

She put the picture in the box.

There would be no more night-before-the-trial negotiating sessions, no more acrimonious teleconferences, no more courtroom wrangling, no more explaining that she was TJ's friend, nothing more and nothing less.

Would there be less friendship tomorrow? Would he hate her? Could he forgive her? Most important, would she succeed? They had had a New York lunch together yesterday—he at his desk across town with pastrami on rye, she at her desk with a chef's salad, their speaker phones on, secretaries told to hold all calls—and she had asked him for the hundredth time to go back home and he had refused.

"Oh, TJ, we gave up too much to be successful," she said quietly. Her neatly manicured hand reached to the desktop for her memo minder—must send paralegal to research whether kidnapping across state lines increases the penalty—before remembering that the memo minder had been retrieved by the office manager on the same visit at which he had given the obligatory reminder that her health benefits could be extended for up to a year after she left the firm.

"Of course, everybody's hoping you'll just come on back before then," he added. "Mr. Greenough said that you needed some time off after that big antitrust case."

That big antitrust case had gobbled up three years of Paige's life. One company suing another, who promptly countersued, which resulted in day-long depositions, complex evidence-gathering, document exchanges, delaying tactics, motion-filing, settlement negotiations—and in the end, the only people who had made money had been the lawyers. Including the partners at Paige's firm. They were extremely pleased with her. And extremely sorry to see her go.

The south hallway of Greenough, Challenger & Redmond's twenty-sixth-floor offices was brightly lit and humming with activity. Secretaries were shutting down their computers, scrambling to get that last typed brief on their bosses' desks, calling to tell their children and husbands what time they'd get home.

Four o'clock in the afternoon was when many lawyers got their second wind—woe to the attorney who wasn't at his desk when Mr. Greenough prowled the halls at seven-thirty!

Paige thought of the hours of her life—gone, all gone—and the Saturdays and Sundays that she had persuaded herself she liked to come into the office because she could get so much work done without the phones ringing. The nights she had canceled dinner dates (not so bad) and given theater tickets to her secretary. (Nelly would call her husband and tell him to hop on the next train into the city.) The two Christmases she had spent reviewing documents for a client instead of with Teddy and Zoe, and her only scheduled vacation, which was canceled the day before because a client had received a merger proposal from a competitor. (Paige had sent Nelly and her husband to Mexico.)

"You sure you don't want me to help you carry this stuff downstairs?" Nelly asked, peering over her cubicle wall. A lively shock of gray hair fell over her face.

"That's okay," Paige said.

"Your mom called again. I told her you were on your way."

"Thanks."

"Your father?" Nelly knew that his condition was one of the reasons Paige wouldn't be coming back.

"Good days and bad days."

"Well, then, goodbye," Nelly concluded awkwardly. "And thank you again. For everything. We put an offer in on the house I told you about. We couldn't have done it without your . . . gift."

Paige shrugged in a way that said it was nothing. Nelly started to cry and Paige put down her box to hug her. The temp in the next cubicle stopped typing. She stared. Paige told Nelly she'd write.

"You'd better," Nelly sniffed. "I hope everything . . . well, everything you're looking for—I hope you find it."

I do, too, Paige thought.

And I hope I don't end up losing my best friend in the process.

"Call me if you need anything," Nelly said, adding as Paige was nearly out of earshot, "But you're never the type that needs anything."

Paige slipped out of the reception area, grateful that the woman at the desk was new. She gave Paige a quizzical look—what attorney would leave the office at this hour?—but said nothing.

The elevator was empty and Paige didn't see anyone she knew when she got out on the second floor of the underground parking garage. She walked over to the tomato-red sports car and put the box in the trunk, remembering to put her briefcase on the passenger seat so that TJ wouldn't get suspicious.

She checked the CD in the player. Johannes Brahms. Quiet and soothing. A can of TJ's favorite soda and the potato chips he had recently become addicted to were in a paper bag behind the passenger seat.

Just what a kidnapper needed to sedate her prey.

Secretaries, fast-food workers, clerks at other law firms, and paralegals were pouring out of the tall, glass-and-steel boxes of Fifty-third Street and the Avenue of the Americas. Although it was only June, heat sizzled up from the sidewalk. Men slung their suit jackets over their shoulders. The construction workers on the corner had obviously been instructed to lay down their tools and perform their function as oglers of passing women. A cabbie hung out of his window to berate a jaywalker in a fierce Baltic language.

Taking a deep breath, Paige pulled the little Spitfire out onto the street.

One thing she wouldn't miss about New York was the traffic. Most of her colleagues didn't bother with cars, preferring cabs, the subway, walking, or calling Paige in an emergency. But Paige wasn't a New Yorker in her heart (where it mattered) and she liked the freedom of a car, remembering fondly when having a pickup truck, a gas station map in the glove compartment, and a couple of girlfriends was all she needed to get her thinking road trip.

Just this morning, she had informed the parking garage three blocks from her apartment building that she was leaving.

"They all do," the garage manager said. "New York ain't no place to raise a kid. It's always the kids that make them leave. Goin' to Connecticut, Westchester, or Long Island?"

"Colorado."

He looked puzzled.

"The state," she prompted.

He allowed as how the Broncos played good ball.

"Good luck to you," he said. "Hey, wait a minute. You don't have a kid. You're the single lawyer-lady. Why are you leaving all this?"

It wasn't a complimentary description, but it was perfectly serviceable and true. And so she shook hands with the men and handed out envelopes with a small but reasonable tip enclosed in each one. She had done the same for the doormen at her apartment building.

"Goodbye, goodbye," she sang as she drove for the last time through midtown. "Goodbye, New York."

On the north side of Thirty-third and Fifth Avenue, she shoved her head up between the steering wheel and the windshield to get one final look at the Empire State Building. She was rewarded with a trumpet blast from the taxi behind her because she took a millisecond too long to respond to the light change.

Forty-five minutes later, she spotted TJ on Wall Street, standing on the curb in front of the headquarters of J.P. Morgan, where he spent his days and most of his nights. He had a cell phone parked on his ear, and when he caught sight of her car, he waved a stack of pink and yellow message slips as a hello. She couldn't help but smile.

"So who's this mysterious client?" he asked, sliding into the seat beside her. He hung up the phone and put it in his suit jacket pocket but it rang again. "Sorry. I'll turn it off right after this call."

Paige said nothing. She didn't like the phone. Didn't like the little message slips that he had put in the coffee-cup holder between them. Didn't like the briefcase bulging with paperwork. Didn't like the laptop that followed him everywhere—but which, she noted, must have been left at the office with a bone, a bowl of water, and some newspaper.

It was okay for him to bring the rest of his office pets. This was one time that the phone, the slips, and the briefcase would work in her favor.

"It's okay," she mouthed silently. At the next light, she reached across his seat and put her finger on the recliner.

"Hold on," he said to his caller. He put his finger on MUTE but she shook her head.

"You might as well get comfortable. Traffic is terrible."

"Sorry about the call," he said. "The market is going wild."

"No, it's okay. Get your work done. I understand."

He stretched out his legs—normally her car, any car, required him to sit like a child with his knees up close to his chest. But she had put the seat as far back as it could go. She pulled out the can of his favorite soda and put it in the passenger-side cup holder.

He nodded in gratitude even as he told his caller that movement in the Japanese markets wasn't going to make any difference in this transaction.

She put on the Brahms. Very soft. Very, very soft and soothing.

In this warm and quiet cocoon, the two friends lurched north through Tribeca. Paige hoped to make the Holland Tunnel before he started with his questions.

TWO

"So who's this client?" TJ asked, tossing the multicolored slips into his briefcase. "You sounded so damned mysterious."

He leaned across the coffee-cup holder to kiss her cheek. He always kissed her cheek. So chaste. And slapped her palm. So buddy-buddy. Next he would give her the once-over and frown. He always told her that she was never going to get a man if she dressed like a frump.

"Yeah, and I'm never going to be taken seriously as a lawyer if I dress like a showgirl," she always replied.

But today he was on the all-important trail of a new client. That trumped any personal observations. He slipped his cell phone into the ashtray.

"Why the mystery?"

"I was mysterious because he's mysterious."

"But wealthy?" he asked, yawning.

Good sign, yawning.

"Oodles and oodles of money," Paige replied. "And he needs a lawyer—that'd be me—to manage his estate matters. And a financial advisor—that'd be you—to make his money into more money."

"And how come I've never heard of him before?"

"Because he's a recluse. He won't come to either of our offices."

"So we're going to his office?" He glanced around, suspicious of the Tribeca streets. Millionaires didn't rent office space around here.

"No. His house."

Calculating. His jaw shot up. Central Park West, perhaps, but then why was she taking a left on Canal Street? Paige knew he was just about to ask why they were heading for the Holland Tunnel.

"And where is his house?"

TJ's phone rang.

"Go ahead," Paige said blithely. "It's okay."

Got her out of the questioning. Got her out of the lying. She wasn't good at lying. Didn't do it often enough, even in her professional life. Never wanted to get into the habit.

"Haven't seen you in a while," TJ said when the call was over. "When was it? Last month?"

She nodded. New York friendships were like that, and theirs was a very New York friendship. A phone call or E-mail once or twice a week. Brunch on Sunday morning if neither of them was going into the office—or if TJ didn't have a girlfriend in his bed—or if one of them wasn't out of town on business. Which worked out to once a month. Dinners were canceled for clients coming in, for deadlines, and for bosses inviting one or the other out for drinks.

But they were loyal friends in the ways that mattered. TJ was the one who cut out of work and brought Tylenol, tabloids, and chicken soup from the corner deli when she was sick. Paige helped him shop for just the right gift when a girlfriend's birthday loomed. When

Paige won her first case, TJ was at the courthouse steps with champagne. When she broke up with her first boyfriend, TJ was at her apartment in twenty minutes with Chinese food and sympathy.

"Your hair's different," he said, touching the ends. "Less severe. I like it."

"I'm just overdue for a haircut. You look like you got a tan. Is this from the weekend in Barbados?"

"Yeah. Wish you would have taken off work."

"A romantic weekend in Barbados by definition does not include three people."

"She was a bore."

"So you said."

"You would have been more fun."

"Naturally, but when the woman in question's greatest accomplishment is having a month named after her, I don't think it's a fair competition. What was she? Miss January?"

"April."

"Does this mean the SunOil heiress . . . ?"

"She doesn't care about whether I see other women."

"So you say."

The phone rang.

"Take it," she urged.

"What did you say this guy's name was?" TJ asked a few minutes later when he hung up the phone.

She was ready for this one.

"Rockefeller. You've heard of the Rockefeller family."

"Very funny. All right, which one is this guy?"

"A cousin. First name's John, and he's the cousin of the New York John Rockefeller."

"Which John? The New York, New York, John or his son, the Albany, New York, John?"

"I don't know, but this guy married into the Du-Pont family," Paige added to put TJ off track. She felt his mind, his doubt, his cynic's muscle flexing. "TJ, look. I need your help because if I get this client I'll have my partnership review nailed down. You know how much I want to make partner."

Paige knew that the appeal for TJ to help her in her career, in her climb to a corner office in Greenough, Challenger & Redmond was powerful. So powerful that it distracted him from asking too many questions she couldn't answer.

Such as: Which John Rockefeller and which Du-Pont? After all, there was an inch-thick layer of Rockefeller heirs throughout New York and the Northeastern states. And as for DuPonts, the state of Delaware boasted thousands—all of them no doubt at this very moment gathering at checkout lines in convenience stores, demanding to cash dividend checks made on oil, petroleum products, and plastic.

TJ's head swiveled as he caught sight of an unfamiliar street sign. When he was on the phone he hadn't noticed how far out of the financial district they were, but now . . . What were they doing in New Jersey?

"How long will it be before we get there?"

"Oh, a good hour."

TJ groaned. An hour away from his office was as good as forever. The Dow could tumble, the Federal Reserve crumble—after all, they were made of hot air and confidence.

"And where did you say he lived?"

"Look, TJ. I really want to land this client," Paige continued, seeming not to have heard his question. "Please don't be upset about the time."

"You're my best friend, Paige. It's cool."

"You're a great friend, too." Paige relaxed her grip on the steering wheel.

TJ felt vaguely uncomfortable with the praise of his friendship, thinking as he often did that there wasn't another woman on earth that he didn't think of as a bedmate first, a dinner partner second and a friend—well, not at all, not really.

He looked at Paige's suit again and noted how it concealed every possible evidence of feminine curve. How even the pearl buttons on her silk blouse looked like the doorknobs on a maximum-security prison. He had always been a man who thought of women's hair as meant for his caress, but Paige's short, straight, severe bob made not a neuron twitch in his fingers. He had no—absolutely no—desire to run his fingers through it. Her makeup—what little there was—made her look older than twenty-eight. But then, most cosmetics did that to a woman.

All in all, Paige wasn't a man magnet. It wasn't that she wasn't beautiful or that she was unfriendly to the male species. And she had had a boyfriend or two, although TJ never liked any of 'em. Hadn't minded telling 'em. They never lasted.

Maybe the reason he and Paige could be friends was that, after that one night—just one night—she had become the most unsexual person he knew. It wouldn't have worked otherwise. So he'd let her wear the suits, the severe haircut, even the matronly pink lipstick.

"Okay, I'm cool about the time but you drive me back to the office immediately afterward," he said. She nodded. "Aw, Paige, you know how happy I am to do this. Especially after refusing to go to the reunion. I feel guilty that I'm letting you down. Isn't it this coming weekend?"

"Uh, yeah, I guess so," Paige said, adding a nonchalant lift of her shoulder. "I don't have the invitation with me."

Liar, liar, pants on fire! The invitation to the Sugar Mountain High School Reunion was in her suitcase, locked in the trunk.

"Can't believe you'd want to go back there. Hick town. Nothing to do."

"I want to see my son. And Katherine and Zoe. And you have your family."

Silence.

"So go," TJ finally said.

"Signing this client is more important," she said. "If it turns out he needs work done this week and into the weekend—well, there goes the reunion."

"That's my Paige. Wall Street Tiger."

"Avenue of the Americas."

"Well, Avenue of the Americas Tiger doesn't have quite the same ring to it."

The phone rang again, but TJ turned off the power and loosened his tie. The car was warm, cozy warm, and the sun was playing hide-and-seek behind the clouds. Funny how good it felt to yawn.

"Do you mind if I close my eyes for a bit?"

She had been banking on his being tired. He worked such long hours that he was capable of falling asleep in minutes and yet, waking, he would be all smiles and sharpness. Last night he had taken a conference call from a consortium of Japanese investors. It had run from two A.M. to four A.M. At least that was what his secretary had told Paige.

Sleepiness would work in her favor.

"Take a little nap," Paige suggested. "Do you want the music on or off?"

"It's okay either way." TJ shrugged. "I really like, uh, really enjoy this music. It's by . . ."

It was unlike him not to know what was playing, whether rock or country or classical.

"It's Brahms," Paige said, glancing at him.

He was asleep, with his mouth relaxed in a half smile. A single pink message slip fluttered to the floor. His crisp white shirt strained against a rhythmic breath. The tiny lines etched at the corners of his eyes became more prominent as he relaxed.

A light rain began to fall as she crossed the border into Pennsylvania. She had a full tank of gas. A six-pack of soda loaded with caffeine on the floor behind her seat. Change for the toll booths. And a little more than two thousand miles to go.

She had planned this with the precision she used in her office. She had picked this day because she knew he had taken that overnight conference call—so he'd fall asleep quickly. She had used her key to his co-op and packed the essentials he'd need for a week—no use having to stop for razors and tooth-brushes. At her own apartment, she'd packed every suit but one in a box that she dropped off at a charity that distributed suits to welfare recipients preparing for job interviews. She'd changed the oil in her car, checked the air pressure on the tires, plotted her course on a map so that she would not have to break momentum to ask for directions.

But though Paige and the National Weather Service had anticipated a thunderstorm would swing through Virginia, neither had foreseen the cumulonimbus clouds veering east and then suddenly taking a whimsical detour into southern Pennsylvania. Traffic on Interstate 76 crawled along. Trucks and cars pulled over to the shoulder to wait out the storm. Paige exited at U.S. 222, short of Harrisburg. She needed gas, some coffee, food, and a bathroom.

"Paige," TJ said when he woke.

"What?"

He cleared his throat. "Where are we? The truth."

Truth? It was time for it already?

"Pennsylvania. Lancaster County."

A sharp intake of breath barely audible against the *flish-swooosh-flish-swoosh* of the windshield wipers.

She peered ahead, straining to see beyond her headlights. She had studied the map—the exit at 222 was supposed to lead onto a frontage road filled with fast food joints and motels. But fourteen miles had netted nothing but darkness.

She pulled over to the shoulder.

"How long have I been asleep?"

"Four-and-a-half hours."

She saw the barest blue outline of his face in the reflection of a lightning strike. He didn't look angry exactly. Just puzzled. He cleared his throat.

"There's no client, is there?"

"No."

"No DuPonts, no Rockefellers, no rich recluses with money."

"I'm sorry."

"Maybe you'd better tell me why I'm here."

"TJ, it's about that reunion."

He uttered an oath. Loud. Clear. Four lettered.

And then he opened the car door. A *whoosh* of rain and cool air hit her before he slammed the door. He strode out into the grass just beyond the head-lights, holding his head in his hands. Paige put her finger on the automatic-window button. Better than following him. If she followed him, they might end up in a game very similar to musical chairs and he might get the driver's seat. She poked her head out the window. The rain was wet, cold, but it felt good and clean.

"TJ, get back in the car."

That oath again. She didn't like it when he swore, which he didn't do nearly as often as most traders on the New York Stock Exchange. Maybe today he was just trying to fill his quota of bad words for the month.

"Not until I cool off!" he shrieked, uttering three more four-lettered words. "I'm angry, Paige. Very angry. Boiling hot angry. Furious angry. Angry angry."

She shrugged and closed the window. She would be patient. She pulled out the trucker's atlas, turned to the page devoted to Pennsylvania, and tried to figure out where they were.

He got back in, bringing the odor of rain, grass, and dirt with him. He dripped and he made no apology for the water. She closed the atlas but left on the light at the rearview mirror.

"Paige, I've got a multimillion-dollar deal cooking with the Japanese. I've got the SunOil merger in Chicago, which is the biggest deal in my life. I've got a half dozen clients who think I'll be in the office tomorrow and—you know what?—I am going to be there."

"But you won't be."

"Won't be what?"

"In the office."

"Oh, yes, I will. You're going to turn this car around and drive me back into Manhattan. Right now."

He patted the front of his suit jacket. Kicked his feet around the floor of the passenger side. Opened the glove compartment. Closed it.

"And where the hell is my cell phone?"

"I threw it out the window a half hour out of New York."

He stared at her. That phone was his lifeline.

"Paige, you're ruining me."

She said nothing.

"Drive me back."

"No, TJ."

"I'll get a cab."

"Plenty of 'em," she said.

They both peered out into the dark, rainy night.

The empty road.

"Okay, you don't have to rub it in. Why don't you drive us to the nearest gas station, restaurant, anything? I'll call my secretary. Damn it, Paige, you are the most sensible, levelheaded, rational woman I have ever known. But this reunion thing has got you acting like a raving lunatic."

She started the car and pulled out onto the rain-slicked road.

"I told you I didn't want to go and I meant it," he continued. "You go. Have a great time. You remember all those people from high school. You'll have a blast. And you can tell me about it when you get back to the city. But leave me out of it."

Paige pulled into the gravel drive of the Get Some Sleep Inn, which consisted of a chalet-style office, six brick cabins forming a semicircle around a black-top parking lot, and an ice chest. The skeletal lines of a neon sign were dark but legible—this inn featured television in every cabin and checkout time wasn't until noon. The windows of the six little cabins were dark. A row of spotlights arranged to illuminate the chalet's facade was dead. A single pale flame of candlelight appeared in the chalet's window.

"What is this?" TJ said.

"A motel."

"I know that. But is it open?"

"They have cars."

A car was parked in the space directly in front of five of the cabins. A forbidding sign on the empty parking space declared that it was reserved for occupants of cabin six.

"TJ, do you remember the LSATs?"

He shrugged. "You took the LSATs. I didn't."

"Do you remember why I took them?"

"Because you can't get into law school without taking the LSATs."

"Yeah, but who filled out the form, sent in the money, and dragged me out of bed to drive me to the test site?"

"Me," he said, unrepentant. "I knew you would make a great lawyer. I was right."

"And do you remember how I got my job at Greenough?"

"You interviewed for it."

"Because you called up Walter Greenough, who happened to be the father of a girl you were dating at the time."

"I dated his daughter? Oh, yeah, I remember now. She was kinda cute, but wanted to settle down and make babies."

"Don't change the subject. You got me that job, and do you remember what I said when I got the offer?"

He cleared his throat.

"Uh, no."

"Exactly," she said. "I said no. I didn't want to work there. But you talked me out of no. Told me I'd be shortchanging myself if I didn't practice in the only city in the country that matters."

"You would have been shortchanging yourself."

"When I went into Greenough's office after a week of listening to your nagging, he told me that I had already accepted the job and he had a letter from me on my own stationery. Who wrote that letter?"

He was guilty as charged. "I just didn't want you to let an opportunity like that slip through your fingers."

"Point is, you've done some bold things to get me to do what you wanted. Now it's my turn."

"Yeah, but there's a difference. I did those things for your own good."

Flish-swoosh-flish-swoosh, replied the windshield wipers.

Point made.

"You stay here," TJ growled. "I'll see if they have a phone and a couple rooms. If we have to, we'll stay the night. When you get some sleep, you'll come to your senses. If we get an early start, we can be at my office by nine."

She followed him into the front office under the awning, partly out of concern he might try to rent or outright purchase a car to get back to the city, partly out of fear of being left in the dark night. She put her keys in her suit jacket pocket.

The innkeeper's office was illuminated by a kerosene lamp and three long candles. A silver-haired man in overalls sat behind the desk, hunched over a magazine.

"Evenin', folks. Mighty wicked out there," he said laconically.

"It sure is," TJ agreed. He shoved the door closed behind Paige. "Look. We need a phone."

"Phone service got cut 'bout an hour ago."

"Have you got a cell phone?"

"I like lots of wires with my phones."

TJ groaned.

"What about rooms?" Paige asked.

"Today's your lucky day. We got one left. Cabin six. The Bridal Suite."

"The Bridal Suite?" TJ asked.

"We aren't married," Paige said.

"Then I'll charge you five dollars extra for being illicit." Maybe he winked. Maybe he didn't. Tough to tell in the dark.

"No, you don't understand," Paige said, feeling a shiver of anxiety. Or maybe just cold from the rain. "We can't manage with one room."

"Well, how many do you need?"

"Two."

The man shook his head.

"No can do. Bridal Suite or nothing."

"All right," TJ agreed, pulling his wallet out of his pants pocket. "Bridal Suite."

As he signed in, he looked at Paige.

"We're not sleeping together," she said firmly.

"I wasn't even thinking of that, Paige."

But she had been.

They had nearly ruined a good friendship—on this, they both agreed. Although right now that good friendship might be ruined regardless of the sleeping arrangements.

The desk clerk showed him where to sign and TJ signed their names: Mr. TJ Skylar and Ms. Paige Burleson.

After the clerk refused to take TJ's titanium-plus credit card because it couldn't be verified with the phone lines down, Paige produced cash.

"Thank you, miss, and here, you might want a little midnight snack."

He threw a package of cookies and two soda pops down on the desk. He blew out the candles and gave them to Paige. As he handed TJ the room key, TJ flicked water droplets from his wet lapel.

"You know, son, she's awfully good-looking," he said. "I'd dry her off and reconsider the sleeping-together part. Especially on a night as fearsome as this."

THREE

TJ unlocked the door of the sixth cabin, reflexively flipped the wall switch and got nothing. Nothing but darkness and the bubble gum smell of industrial cleanser. He held out his hand to the darkness, stepping forward cautiously to locate what seemed to be a table or a desk. He put the candles down and rummaged in his pocket for a lighter.

When he had three lit candles sitting upright in a glass ashtray, he took off his sopping wet suit jacket and surveyed his surroundings.

Dominating the room was a bed, looking at first like it might be a twin, until he realized he was so used to space-gobbling king-sized mattresses that he hadn't recognized it as a double. The quilt looked as if bugs were crawling all over it, but on closer examination TJ determined they were red chenille hearts stitched on white duck cloth.

How cute, he thought numbly.

On the desk next to the candles he had lit was a lamp which he tried twice to turn on before he remembered there was no electricity. The cable television was positioned so that it could be watched from the bed. On top of it was an empty ice bucket, a bottle of the very cheapest champagne, and two plastic flutes whose stems were tied with white satin ribbons.

The tiny room allowed for only one chair—pale pink upholstery with emaciated legs and a throw pillow upon which was embroidered "Happiness is Being Married to Your Best Friend".

He rubbed a headache which was forming behind the bridge of his nose.

His best friend closed the door behind her.

"Paige, I'm not happy."

"I know."

He slumped on the bed. Stuck in the middle of nowhere. Okay, Pennsylvania. But same thing, if you considered that he had no phone, no fax, no internet hookup and no electricity. He was missing the conference call with a Japanese firm that looked promising as a client but which would regard his no-show as proof of reckless instability and unsuitability for business. The European markets were opening in—he touched the luminator dial on his watch—an hour and he had no idea if they were up, down, or holding steady.

If he were in his Central Park West apartment, he'd be wearing dry khakis and a cashmere-soft T-shirt. He'd be in front of his computer screen with the speaker phone on. He'd be comfortably taking care of business.

And best of all, he wouldn't be worrying about Paige.

He wasn't angry. Not anymore. At least not much. Couldn't be mad at her. She'd lost her mind. All the stress and worry about making partner must have caught up with her. He watched her closely as she walked to the center of the room, turned to look at the framed poster of a couple embracing beneath a canopy held by plastic angels, and then shrugged.

She didn't look crazy.

But she had definitely fallen over the edge.

One of the guys on his pickup basketball team, a guy he'd known for years, had gotten so wrought up about the invitation to the partnership echelon of his law firm that he'd cracked—simply cracked. And in the space of a week, he had had six anxiety attacks that were fearsome. This buddy had called TJ six times saying he needed a ride to the emergency room because he was having a heart attack. Of course, he wasn't having a heart attack—he was sent home, sheepish and weary, with an admonition to get some rest and perhaps embark on a fitness program. Had TJ ever gotten angry with him? Hell, no. After the sixth attack, TJ had found him the best psychiatrist in Manhattan. And he gave the guy a dinner party at the Athletic Club when he made partner.

TJ still had the phone number of the psychiatrist in his black book.

But Paige didn't need to lie on a couch for two fifty-minute sessions a week while a guy took notes and asked her about her feelings. Knowing Paige, she'd probably sit up and ask the doctor about his.

If TJ had a telephone, the first call he'd make would be to Walter Greenough. He'd beg the respected lawyer to fast-track her partnership consideration. As it was, TJ would try to get her to go to sleep and he'd watch over her to make sure she didn't pull any other crazy stunts. She was his best friend, the only constant in his life. He'd see her through this.

He wiggled his toes. He hadn't noticed being cold, but now he felt it.

It did not dawn on him, even for an instant, that going to their high school reunion was a worthwhile idea.

Paige closed the white curtains against the wind and rain. She held up TJ's weekender bag.

"Here, there're some dry clothes."

He stared.

"You packed for this?"

"Sure," she said. "I packed your favorite jeans, a couple of t-shirts, your Harvard sweatshirt, and socks. Your feet must be so cold. Go change. Your hiking boots are in here, but you'll probably not want them."

"So it wasn't an impulse thing?"

"Not at all. I've been planning for this ever since you told me that Times Square would sprout corn-fields before you'd go back to Sugar Mountain."

He shook his head, staring blankly as she opened her duffel bag. She pulled out a pair of flannel pa-jamas, a toothbrush, and bunny slippers. The ones she wore when she worked at home. Hers or his.

"Now if you're not going to use the bathroom, I call dibs," she said.

She left him to cautiously look through his weekender. She had thought of everything—clothes, toiletries, even the latest Tom Wolfe book that he had gotten last Christmas and never opened. Or was it the Christmas before last?

She had left an invitation on the chair. The same

invitation he had ripped in half when he found it in his mailbox.

In Sugar Mountain this weekend, there'd be a parade with a float for past and present members of the football team. No way he'd be on the float—it had only been because Coach Scandaglia had said he'd be second-stringed if he didn't that he had endured being on the float when he was in high school.

There'd be a cocktail party where the elementary school kids would sing school songs—tra la la, Sugar Mountain, tra la la. He couldn't remember the anthem, except for the fact that it was stupid. Had he ever been so young that he had sung for the generation before him? Because he was always the tallest, he had always been put in the back and told to sing lower than dogs could hear.

There'd be a big party—their class was ten years out, but Sugar Mountain was so small that all the reunions were grouped together in the school gym. And then the mayor would invite everyone back to his bar for a drink—and his brand of country funky music, with the mayor himself on trumpet.

Friday, Saturday, Sunday. If he went with Paige there wasn't any way of getting back to Manhattan until next Monday at the earliest.

A week out of the office to go to a high school reunion? He'd never spent a week out of the office, and he wasn't starting now. Couldn't start now. Not if he was going to get the Japanese deal settled. Not if he was supposed to be in Chicago in two days to settle SunOil.

What if she were dead set on going to the reunion? There was no law against going to your high school reunion. No law against it, except the law against stupidity. He'd pretty much always been able to talk her into or out of anything—but if she wanted this, hell, let her go.

But TJ Skylar back on Sugar Mountain?

"No way," he said aloud.

"What did you say?"

She had emerged from the bathroom in baggy flannel pj's and slippers. Her rain-slicked hair was combed neatly behind her ears. The lipstick was gone and her lips were surprisingly pale.

"Nothing," he said. He had a sudden insight. "Paige, does this have to do with your biological clock?"

"I will not honor that question with a reply."

"No, really, I was reading an article in a magazine my secretary had on her desk. You're twenty-eight. You're thinking about having babies. You're thinking that you're going to go to your reunion and reignite something. I just never figured you for having any kind of . . . well, I always thought Teddy was Kate's son, and so I thought you felt bad because you wanted a son who was your own."

His words fell limp in the face of her withering glare.

"What you know about women couldn't fit into a teacup. That's why I always have to advise you."

"I know what they want."

"Then how come you can't hang on to one for more than a few months?"

He reared back defensively.

"Any one of the women I've been with would have married me. Several of them asked, and I've tried to be real sensitive when I say no to a proposal because, frankly, I figure it must be damn harder to work up the courage to ask a man than it is for a man to ask a woman. You got it wrong, sister. It's you that's always needed my advice about men."

"Your advice consists of saying 'he's a jerk' about any man who has more than one date with me."

"I can't help it if you have bad luck with men."

"And of course, the ever helpful *why don't you buy some of the underwear in this catalogue?*"

"It would help you get a second date with a decent guy if you were a little less . . . businesslike in your . . . intimate attire."

"Why would any man be in a position to see my intimate attire on a first date?"

"You've got a point," he said.

"And when do you see my intimate apparel?"

"Well, never."

"Exactly."

Paige shoved a bundle of clothes into the garbage can.

"I've been tempted," TJ said quietly.

"No, you haven't. But thanks for saying you have."

The room was lit by a single candle, but the shadows were not so dense that he didn't see her suit and silk blouse shoved into the garbage can.

"Don't you want to hang those up?"

"I won't be needing them."

"Yeah, you will. Next week."

"All right, fine."

She took out the suit, the pearl-buttoned silk blouse, and the sensible pumps. Folded them very carefully and stacked them neatly on the desk.

"That's better," he said. "For a minute I thought you were going to tell me you weren't ever going back to New York. Now that would make me throw you over my shoulder and walk back to New York tonight!"

"Lucky thing I'm going to sleep, huh?"

In the bathroom, he changed into jeans and a t-shirt and rubbed the dampness out of his hair. When he brushed his teeth, he actually felt relaxed. He had slept longer than he usually allowed himself. He hadn't heard a phone ring or a fax machine burp in hours. The ping! of Internet Explorer telling him that he had a new message was just a distant memory.

He brought the candle out into the room with him.

She was sitting on the bed eating cookies.

In the middle of the bed.

"Move over," he said.

"No," she said.

He looked down. The light wasn't good but it was enough so he could see the carpet wasn't plush.

"I don't think we should sleep together," Paige added.

"Where am I going to sleep?"

"On the floor."

"Come on. We're adults. We can sleep in the same bed."

She looked doubtful.

"Paige, I'm involved with someone."

She made a face.

"I know you don't like Shawna. But she's very nice."

"Then how come you keep breaking up?"

"Because, well, I don't know."

"She's got such nice qualities. Big breasts, blond hair, big breasts, the personality of a kitten, big breasts and a father who owns the largest oil refinery in America. Did I mention big breasts?"

He sighed.

"Okay, look, you're not doing any better in the romance department. You know, I was thinking about what you said—I haven't said every man you've been out with is a jerk. In fact, I've set you up with perfectly wonderful men on three occasions."

"All nebbishes," Paige corrected. "Arrogant nebbishes."

"Then how come each of them got married to the next woman they dated after you?"

"There are so few available men in New York that are straight, working, and haven't served time in prison," Paige said, dusting crumbs off the quilt. "Any nebbish with a credit card and a tie thinks he's a catch."

He peered at the end of the bed. She had laid out for him a pink wool blanket and a single white pillow with the word *Groom* embroidered in delicate silk thread.

"Can I at least sit on the bed? I'll keep my feet on the floor if it'll make you feel better. In fact, I can guarantee you that I'm not even going to sleep."

"Then you won't mind sitting over there."

They both looked at the singularly uncomfortable-looking chair.

Happiness is Being Married to Your Best Friend.

"Are you making me sleep on the floor because I said I was tempted to make love to you? Because I take it back. I've never, ever wanted to make love to you. I mean since . . . well, you know."

"I know you haven't. You've never once acted as if you have. But you're still sleeping on the floor."

He grimaced.

"I think the owners of this motel must have planned this bridal suite so that the only place that's comfortable is under the sheets."

"They did a good job, didn't they?" Paige said, stretching like a satisfied cat.

"I thought our relationship was one of complete and utter equals. No accounting for archaic sex roles. Buddies. Just buddies. Why can't we flip a coin?"

"Because I'm still the woman," Paige pointed out. She popped the last cookie into her mouth and crumpled the package. "Sweet dreams."

"Look, Paige, one last thing. We're going back to New York tomorrow."

"Is there a bus that passes through here?"

"I don't know. We'll take your car."

"Don't count on it."

She crouched up on her knees and pulled her pj top up just high enough so that he could see the milky white flesh of her stomach. And the silver dog-tag chain around her waist. On it was her car key. She dropped the hem of her top.

"Good night," she said.

And she flopped back down on the bed in a distinctly unwelcoming diagonal position. With the white quilt up over her head.

He waited for her to reconsider, to come to her senses, to do the considerate thing—which was always her manner.

She wouldn't, couldn't fall asleep knowing that he was uncomfortable and that she had it within her power to change that.

Or could she?

FOUR

He sat on the chair, but the chair complained. He picked up the telephone—just in case—but the phone was dead. He crouched next to the candles, but they didn't throw off enough light for him to read the Welcome to Lancaster County brochure, much less the report from his intern about emerging plastics markets in Thailand.

Assuming he had the energy to go out in the rain to retrieve his briefcase from Paige's car and find the report. He got up and pulled back the curtain—it was still wicked rain out there. But what was he thinking? He'd have to get the car key. He looked back at the bed. The key was on a chain around her waist. Her tiny, flat-stomached waist. Her vanilla sweet-smelling flesh never touched by the sun, flesh as pale as a moon lily. As soft as . . .

"Stop thinking like that," he said aloud.

The last time he had been in a bedroom with Paige, they had nearly screwed up everything that made them good friends. They had agreed—never again. And the friendship had survived. Thrived. It was a great surprise to him, because he had never thought men and women could be friends.

He couldn't remember the name of the first girl

Vivian Leiber

he dated when he got out of Harvard Business School, couldn't have said where she worked or if she worked or if she were tall or short. And the next few years—and women—were pretty much the same blurry, ill-defined memory. But he always knew, always in his heart, that Paige was his friend.

The kind of friend he could count on.

And he would always be the friend she could count on, too. Even if she were acting mighty strange about this reunion.

"You know, Paige, I don't go out with as many women as you think. Or even as many as that gossip columnist from the *New York Post* thinks," he said, leaning back against the chair until the chair cried uncle. "Lately, I've been kind of bored—yeah, really, bored with women. Doesn't that sound strange? Bored with them. Or maybe just tired. I've been wondering if it's maybe a medical problem. Or a psychological problem. I feel I should be happier, since I did all this work to become a success. I think I'm a success, right?"

He leaned toward the bed, listening intently for a break, a pause, a hesitation in the rhythmic whisper-soft breath.

"I know you're asleep," he said, taking a chance on sitting on the bed. Carefully, so carefully that she wouldn't awaken. "But you know what, Paige? You're a wonderful friend even when you're asleep. I'll try not to be too angry about being kidnapped. But I'm still not going back to Sugar Mountain. Anyhow, Shawna's gotten it into her head that when a man gets bored with being a bachelor, well, there's really only one cure. Marriage. Trouble is, I've never fallen in love—fallen, off balance, out of control, jumping off a cliff into amour. You haven't either, have you? I don't think that guy from France counts. You were infatuated and he was . . . well, he was looking for a green card. And another thing, you really do take up the whole bed."

She rolled over, confirming his opinion.

He could try for that little corner that wasn't taken up with long legs and a beautiful body—but no, that would be courting trouble.

He eased off the bed, blew out the candles, and wearily sat on the cover she had placed on the floor. The carpet was scratchy and had no give to it. The pillow was too hard, every thread which formed the word *Groom* boring into the back of his head like a drill press.

Of course, he wouldn't go to sleep. After all, he had just gotten nearly five uninterrupted hours of snooze. He'd have to lie all night in the dark. Listening to the rain and smelling the soft familiar vanilla scent that was his best friend.

No, he'd never sleep.

It would be a long night.

A very . . . very . . . very . . . long . . . night.

And a very . . . very . . . long veil.

The woman approaching him wore a frothy white veil. A white gown with embroidered flowers or buttons—or maybe those were little pieces of popcorn on a low neckline. She carried a bouquet of flowers. Or apples. Or maybe it was cotton candy.

He noticed he wore a tuxedo. And the puffy white outlines of his dream morphed into a church. Those really were flowers in the woman's hand. And a banner over the altar said *Happiness is Being Married to . . .*

He was getting married! He felt a smidgen of wonder, idle curiosity really; who was his bride? In fact, he felt some anxiety about her identity because Shawna's father, the president of SunOil, was standing right beside him, a wide grin crowding all the features on his face. But the bride might not be Shawna. There was that model from Italy he saw every few months—whenever her schedule allowed. Or maybe the woman from the futures market—she never seemed to mind that there wasn't a future for them; but oh, boy, had he asked her to marry him?

He needed Paige here. She would tell him whom he was marrying. And how could he get married without his best friend here anyhow? She'd have to be his best man—er, woman.

He glanced around the church, seeing buddies from college, clients, the guy who worked behind the counter at the convenience store in the lobby of his office. He saw his secretary, the mail room manager, several professors from business school. But no Paige.

She was late, he decided. Late for his wedding. And she was ordinarily such a reliable friend. He felt annoyed with her.

He tried to tell the minister that they couldn't start without Paige, but the music was too loud.

He reached out his hand to lift the woman's veil. Surely she wouldn't mind his just getting clear on her identity since Paige wasn't here to help him.

* * *

"Tell the ten o'clock I unexpectedly got called out of town. Reschedule for next week. Tell Charlie to do my ten-thirty meeting; he's not that busy and he just needs to take notes. Ask Fritz to take my eleven o'clock to lunch—doesn't he speak German? I think they're from the German-speaking part of Switzerland; and if they are, get Fritz to take care of them. Then stall my two o'clock. I'll be back by then . . . Where am I?"

TJ pulled back the curtains and stared at nothing. Well, nothing but green fields, a two-lane highway, and a quartet of cows. The cows chewed and stared. Didn't cows have sense enough to get off the road? And windmills. There had to be six windmills in his line of vision—and not one satellite dish.

"I'm somewhere past civilization, in Pennsylvania. If I see one, I'll bring you back a snow globe."

Paige stretched, opening her eyes to brilliant sunlight streaming in the picture window. Outside, she heard a family squabbling as they packed up a station wagon—the father's low baritone, the mother urging children to hurry, a trio of whiners. TJ stood at the desk, shaking his head as he listened to his secretary outlining the fifteen or twenty emergencies that required his immediate attention.

"Tell your secretary that you'll be back next Monday," Paige said and, yawning magnificently, she rolled over on her stomach. She glanced behind her.

TJ stared at her. With that look. That pitying look. He thought she was crazy. And maybe she was, a little. He thought she needed his help. And maybe she did, a little. But she had had enough—enough of the breakneck pace, the incessant one-upmanship, the rudeness, the noise, the smells—enough, enough, enough of the city, of her so-called life!

And enough of lingering in TJ's shadow. She had followed him to Harvard. Spent three years in the law school while he studied across campus at the business school. When he got a job on Wall Street, she took the offer from Greenough, Challenger & Redmond. When he bought a summer home on Long Island, she spent her summer weekends in his guest room—the weekends she didn't have paperwork that couldn't be brought to the beach.

Buddies, pals, best friends.

They were better than lovers.

At least that's what they had always told themselves.

TJ thought it was enough. To be in New York, to chase the dollar, to measure the days in profit made. Well, it wasn't enough. And since she was leaving New York anyhow, she would do the one thing that he needed done more than anything else, the one thing that only a best friend would do.

She'd take him home. Maybe he'd see. Maybe he'd come to his senses. Maybe he'd see that she was needed at home.

And besides, she had promised his mother she'd bring him with her. And promises made to a mother were sacred.

"I'm doing my best to get back to the office," he said into the phone. "I'll call you if I'm going to be late for the two o'clock appointment. What's that about the SunOil people?"

Paige slipped out of bed, sauntered to the window, watched the divisive family get into the station wagon and squeal out of the parking lot. Swerving to avoid the stately cows. She glanced over her shoulder, noticed TJ watching her as he nodded—funny how he thought his secretary could hear his nods—and then she decided she'd better get dressed.

In the bathroom she splashed cold water on her face and was surprised when she looked up at her reflection. A tension that ordinarily manifested itself in a single stern worry line between her brows was gone. No line. No tightness around her lips either. Her lips were full and pink. She rubbed a finger across them—not even chapped, as they usually were because she bit her lips when she was nervous.

Put this in a jar and sell it, she thought. The fountain of youth. Quitting New York. Quitting your job. Quitting the breakneck speed.

She put on her jeans and a simple tank t-shirt, a bra and panties that were so much more comfortable than panty hose. And the difference between sneakers and high heels? FUH-GEDD-ABOUT-IT!

He was waiting for her, briefcase neatly packed, when she emerged from the bathroom. At least he hadn't changed into his suit. Now came the hard part. Getting him to sit down and listen, really listen, to her.

"Let's find some coffee," she said.

He gaped at her.

"Aren't you going to put a shirt on?"

She looked down at herself. A pair of jeans, old and so infrequently worn that they tugged a little tight on her womanly curves. After all, when she was nineteen, she had been built like a pencil. Even so, the jeans weren't what had him mesmerized. No, his wide eyes were glued to the white knit tank top embroidered at its neckline with a dainty bouquet of taffeta flowers.

Admittedly a low neckline, but the straps covered her bra's; and while she would confess she was dressed a bit more provocatively and casually than she would ever allow herself at the office or, frankly, anywhere in New York, she was not in the office and not in New York. And she wasn't going back. Ever.

So she could dress exactly as she pleased.

Which meant: Pantyhose, never again! Suits, not in this lifetime! Scratchy tweeds, no way! And high heels, not on this gal's feet!

And if she wanted to wear a sleeveless t-shirt on a hot summer day . . . even if she took over as president of her father's bank, she'd dress as she pleased. Casual day every day. If she persuaded TJ to help her, he could ditch those pricey English suits.

"You've had girlfriends who could put together an entire wardrobe out of less fabric than I've got on right now."

"Yeah, but those were girlfriends."

"This is beyond talking about," she snapped. "Let's go across the street. There's a diner. We'll have coffee and talk rationally. About the reunion."

He followed her, shoving her silk blouse in his jean's back pocket. Its sleeves hung down past his knees.

He caught her over-the-shoulder disapproval—it had an unsettling effect on him. Not wholly unlike what he would feel if he were the subject of a come-on from a cover model.

FIVE

"Why are you bringing that with you?" she asked, staring at the silk blouse curling its sleeves around the legs of his jeans.

"You might get cold."

"You're my friend, TJ. Not a grunting Neanderthal."

Yeah, sure, but why did he feel like one?

The motel parking lot was empty and the breakfast rush at the diner across the street was long gone. Four men in overalls lingered over their coffee, indistinguishable except for the four different feed company logos on their baseball caps. A waitress in a pink dress and a white ruffled apron cleared tables into a gray plastic bin.

The four men looked up and then went back to their yack-fest. The waitress glanced up from her work. Nobody seemed shocked at Paige's bare pink shoulders or the glimpse of cleavage. Not one of the restaurant patrons swooned at the scent of vanilla that rose from her breasts. Not a soul did a double take at the round full hips that went boom-boom-boom at her every step.

Paige slid onto a red vinyl-and-chrome stool at the counter. TJ sat beside her, glancing this way and that for what reason he could not have said. Through a window to the kitchen, they watched a burly cook lazily scraping the grill with a spatula. He sang a German hymn, lingering at the bass notes and pulling vibrato on the high ones. He didn't spare a glance at his new customers, but TJ would have been ready with a distinctly unfriendly look.

Paige took a stopwatch out of her pocket.

"What's that for?"

"Five minutes. You hear me out. No interrupting."

"Paige, I never interrupt you."

"That's because I always stop talking whenever you start."

"Oh. I didn't know that."

"Coffee?" the waitress asked. She sloshed java into their cups and dropped two menus in front of them. TJ nodded his gratitude. He had always considered the people who claimed to not be fit company until a first cup of coffee as weak and inclined to look for excuses—but overnight he had apparently become one.

He gulped half a cup, enjoying the distracting burn on his tongue. When he placed his cup on the saucer, the waitress poured more.

"We'll need a few minutes," Paige said.

"Take your time." The waitress shrugged. "I got tables to bus."

"Do I get any rebuttal time?" TJ asked, feeling his confidence return.

"You can have your five minutes when I'm done."

She took a deep breath. When her lungs filled, her breasts rose up against the neckline of her dainty top. He glanced at the men in the booth, but they were laboring over the finer points of feed grains. They didn't spare a glance at Paige.

"We work too hard. We don't have a life outside the office. We . . . TJ, what are you staring at?"

He met her eyes guiltily.

"Okay, hand me the blouse," she said.

He whipped it out of his pocket and she put it on. "I'll begin again."

He looked straight into her apple-green eyes. After all, the show was over.

"You know, TJ, you see me in a bathing suit every summer."

"And every summer, you buy the same suit. It's black and it covers everything a bathing suit can cover without being called a pantsuit. And I always have a girlfriend that I'm looking at."

"Because your girlfriends always favor thong bikinis," Paige wearily completed his thought. "Thong bikinis use up all your available attention span."

He fixed the strap of her tank top which had pulled away from her bra strap. Which was black, in high contrast to the white shirt. That she would wear black underwear was oddly disturbing. He shoved his elbows on the counter and stared at his coffee cup as if coffee were the most interesting invention since the mood ring.

"I don't think this is such a good thing," he concluded. He ground his jaws together.

"What? My being a woman?"

"No, your being different. Now, what I'm telling you, I'm telling you as your best friend. You're going to attract a lot of attention."

"You mean male attention. And why is that such a bad thing?"

"Because the way you're dressed, you're going to attract the wrong kind of male attention. You're going to be fending off men who're not interested in a woman's intelligence, but are interested in . . ."

"In what?"

"Dragging her by her hair to their caves."

"I think you're worried because you're always the one with a girlfriend or even more than one girlfriend and I'm always the one who's unattached."

"You've had boyfriends."

"Not many."

"True, but I'd be happy for you if you had a nice boyfriend. But he'd have to be nice. And I don't think nice guys like their women displaying their bodies like this. Paige, this craziness of yours goes beyond just quitting your job and dragging me along for the ride."

Paige sighed.

"Look, don't feel bad. In a way, it's a good thing that I noticed," he said. "I was getting worried."

"About what?"

"Lately, I haven't really had much of an interest in women."

"In women?"

He nodded solemnly.

He thought she'd understand. That he could tell her this one thing, this one troublesome thing so deep within him, this terrible predicament that only a fe-male best friend could be counted on not to interpret as a cry for help—help in the form of a forced trek to a strip joint, a subscription to a girlie magazine, or a mixup with a prostitute.

She opened her mouth, her lips soft and full and touched with red lipstick instead of her usual I-mean-business pink. He thought she was going to sneeze or tell him that she was very sorry and did he want to talk about it?

Instead, she laughed. Laughed so hard, the four men at the table stared with the same blank curiosity as the cows on the road had given him. The waitress stopped counting her tip money to look up. The cook's German hymn died midvibrato.

"I can't imagine," Paige said when she recovered. "You with no interest in women. What about the Oil-Me-Up Girl?"

"Her name is Shawna, by the way."

"I know that."

"And her father is the president of SunOil."

"I know that, too."

"And she's actually a very intelligent girl. Knows a lot about the automotive industry."

That laugh. Beautiful. Musical. The kind of laugh that made a man wish that he was in on the joke.

But this time the joke was him.

He tried one more time. Because they had to like each other. Shawna and Paige. He couldn't lose his best friend. And Shawna? Well, after the ink was dry on the papers in Chicago, she'd be a part of his life. Forever.

"She likes to read *Harvard Business Review, Automotive News,* and *European Automotive Research Quarterly.*"

Paige's laugh had turned into a giggle and the giggle made her eyes dance and her curves jiggle. Damn, this wasn't working out the way he had expected!

"You might be the only man in America who could say that with a straight face," she said when she recovered. "This is June, right? Now which automobile part is the Oil-Me-Up Girl posing with in the SunOil calendar?"

"A muffler," TJ mumbled into his coffee cup.

"And what automobile part were her legs wrapped around for the month of May?"

"A crank case."

"And you say you like her for her intelligence?"

"I didn't say that."

"And don't you think it's a bit strange that the daughter of the CEO is the one posing in the buff?"

"She wears a body stocking," TJ huffed. Then, a bit deflated, "Yeah, I've always thought it was a little strange. But she sure sells parts."

"I'm so happy for SunOil."

"Meow."

"I'm not being catty. I'm just . . . okay, I don't like her."

"I wish you'd learn to," he said, sighing. "Now what about this five minutes?"

"Oh, yeah."

She punched the stopwatch button.

"Five minutes, TJ, that's all I want. Hear me out." She swallowed. Took another deep breath. He decided he would use his rebuttal time to tell her that she had always looked good in a suit. A tailored suit. Skirt breaking at the knees. Sensible heels.

"We both have worked more Christmases and Easters and Thanksgivings than not," she said. "We've traveled all over the world and never seen the sights. I once went to Hong Kong to negotiate a merger for a client and never once got out of the airport. I bet you've never seen Big Ben or Piccadilly Circus in all the times you've been to London."

"Well, actually, I don't really like tourist . . ."

"Don't eat up my five minutes. Point is, we spend a lot of time working. Too much time. And I know it's the only way to get ahead. Especially these days. And that both of us are high achievers—we want to be the best at whatever we do. But we have no life. No life—and we're driving ourselves crazy."

He didn't say a word. Just pointed at her.

"I know. You're saying I'm the one who's crazy. And maybe I am. But when I got the invitation to our reunion weekend, I realized everybody else is going home with a wife or a husband or a baby or some part of themselves that isn't billed to a client or taken as a year-end bonus."

"Is this about your biological clock?"

"Don't ask that again. Well, maybe it is. But if it is, that's a good thing, because I should be thinking about my life. You should, too. About what we value. I don't think either one of us wants to end our lives with a bank account and nothing else. And my parents need me. They're getting older. Dad's mind is a little fuzzy, and Mom has trouble keeping up with the house. They need me. At first, I thought it would be for the weekend. The reunion weekend. See how everybody is, maybe give some thought to what I want to do with my life."

"I thought you were doing with your life what you wanted to do."

"I am. But I'm not. I'm not sure anymore what *I* want and what I want because you want it for me. So I decided to get out of New York."

"For how long out of New York?"

"I'm not sure."

"This reunion has made you crazy."

"Maybe so."

"The damn reunion makes you think everything you've done is worthless and . . ." His face colored. "And then you decide I have to reevaluate my life, too. And you kidnap me!"

"I asked you nicely."

"And I said no."

"I asked you to do it for me."

"I'd do anything for you. Just not this."

"Well, I've thought about why you'd be so determined not to go. Even if I asked you nicely, even if I need your help at home."

"Because Sugar Mountain is a podunk town with absolutely no redeeming features to it. And I have no interest in seeing the people I went to high school with."

"You've said that before."

His eyes darted here and there. Paige knew she was getting close. Very close. Tough to say how he'd react. She glanced at the watch. Just a minute and a half to say what she really needed to say.

"So I ask myself why you would be so adamant. And I think about the fact that you have never, not once in the last eleven years, gone home. Never. Not even for holidays. The holidays you aren't working, that is."

"Paige, don't go there . . ." he warned quietly.

"I have to, TJ. I have to tell you that you've never forgotten. Never forgiven either. You have to go home, TJ; go home so that you can see Jack. And forgive yourself for having lost him. And I have to also tell you that your mother . . ."

He grabbed her keys and bolted out of the diner so fast that the echo of his hands slamming on the counter came second to the cheery bells hung on the door. The four men at the booth stared, their mouths hanging open, their baseball caps bobbing. The cook stopped singing, grunting "What the . . ."

"TJ, wait!" Paige cried, running out into the parking lot.

He strode across the street. Popped open the trunk of her car. Threw his briefcase and weekend bag out onto the pavement with a single, angry jerk.

"TJ, we never talk about Jack. It's always off-limits."

"It's still off-limits."

"See? That proves my point."

He turned on her, pointing a finger in her face, ready to say a lot, and then guiltily shoved his hand in his pants pocket.

"If you're going to start some psychobabble stuff about my needing to go back to Sugar Mountain for some kind of *closure* on my brother's death and that this is going to heal me and make me want to quit my job and be all warm and fuzzy—well, Paige, I think I'll walk all the way back to New York."

"TJ. Please don't."

"Are your five minutes up?"

"I guess. I left the stop watch back at the . . ."

They both glanced at the diner. Four men and a waitress stared out the window.

"Now it's my five minutes," TJ said. "Except it won't take me that long. The reason I left Sugar Mountain is that it's a poor, sniveling excuse of a small town that doesn't have anything going for it. I wanted to make something of myself and I have. I'm proud of my work. I'm proud of who I am."

"Then why won't you go to our reunion? Just for me?"

"Paige Burleson, let me tell you one true thing—I will never again set foot on Sugar Mountain. For you or for anyone or anything else. And I want you to get in the car, turn it around, and head for New York. I'll make it square with Greenough and the law firm; I'll see you through whatever identity crisis you're going through. But I will not go back to Colorado. I'm at the top of my game in the top-of-the-game city."

"Oh, is that it?"

They stood suspended in silence. Even the cows on the road stopped their grumbling disapproval.

"Then this is when we say goodbye," Paige said at last.

He looked as if she had slugged him.

And she had, with those words.

He swallowed. Hard. Searched her face for second thoughts or doubt—but there was nothing but the confidence of a choice made after long thought and sleepless nights. He shook his head, opened his mouth to argue, but she held her ground.

He ran his fingers through his hair.

"Okay. I guess I have to let you do what you're going to do. Goodbye," he said and kissed her cheek. "Are we still friends?"

"Yeah, friends," she said, ducking her head so he wouldn't see the tears.

"Call me when you get . . . there," he said, and they both knew he was avoiding the word *home*.

With his briefcase and weekender in either hand, he walked across the lot to the motel office.

Paige took a ragged breath. She had known this could happen. That her life would have to veer away from his. That she could lose her anchor in him.

"Sorry about kidnapping you!"

"Nada," he said, jerking his briefcase up in a salute. He went into the office.

She closed the trunk of her car. Got into the driver's side, took a deep breath, and put her key in the ignition. And couldn't shake a feeling of gloom that was embedded in her memory from ten years before.

By nightfall, gloom had settled over Sugar Mountain, replacing the shock and horror of the past three days. Dinners were made, picked over, and plates pushed towards the center of the table. Televisions glowed with holiday specials that brought no smiles. Skating parties were canceled. The bridge club women meeting at the Community House threw down their cards and reminisced about long-departed loved ones.

Mothers bathed their children, read them stories, and kissed them with lingering melancholy. Fathers went out back to the shed to check and recheck the fastenings on skis, the clasps on mountain boots, and the tencel wires on homemade sleds.

Mayor Jonathan Stern shook his head wearily when his secretary reminded him that the Christmas tree had been cut down and dragged by tow truck into the village square. He couldn't imagine having the energy to say a few words at the tree-lighting ceremony. He opened the trumpet case after his secretary turned off all the lights and went home. He played slow jazz and drank a bottle of red wine with a deep oaky flavor that seemed to have been made for grieving late into the night.

After shoving the black wool crepe dress in the back of her closet, Paige retreated to the apartment above the garage. It was the first winter in memory that the Burleson family hadn't rented it out to one of the waitresses, trail guides, instructors, and lift operators working at Vail, Breckenridge, and Aspen.

Paige built a fire in the black Ben Franklin stove and tried to concentrate on her homework, a paper due when she returned to college in January. The subject, Eighteenth Century Constitutional Law, had seemed uninteresting enough when assigned. Now— completely irrelevant. She opened her books, read a few sentences, and gave up.

She braided her dark chestnut hair to get it out of her eyes, snagged a cola from the refrigerator, and propped up the pillows on the couch.

She would never be so crass or so proud as to say that she had chosen Harvard University. Rather, Harvard had chosen her. To be sure, the Ivy League school pulled in enough applicants from the East and West

Coasts—and from Chicago's finest high schools—but Rocky Mountain states were sorely underrepresented and Paige's application for early admission had been quickly met with a congratulatory welcome. But Harvard had also chosen Paige in another, more personal way—TJ Skylar was going to Harvard, and where he went, Paige followed.

Watching the flames dance behind the punched iron fireplace screen, Paige wondered if he would go back east after the holidays.

Mayor Stern had brought a bottle of brandy as soon as word of the accident had spread—the demoralized rescue workers had gulped and passed. The minister of Faith Union led a prayer in the Skylar living room which had concluded when he gulped an *amen* and burst into tears. Several women brought hastily made casseroles—but, of course, nobody had an appetite. The two youngest Skylar brothers took turns going upstairs to Mrs. Skylar. Her moans were as plaintive as a coyote's upon the loss of a cub.

TJ sat in an alcove beside the butler's pantry, his face red from wind frost and a bleeding scrape on his forehead that nobody but Paige noticed or cared about. Brambles, dirt, and pine needles clung to his climb suit. His eyes, normally dancing with challenge and confidence, were as dull and murky as day-old coffee. He grunted hello. Using a cocktail napkin she found on the counter in the butler's pantry, she wiped the blood on his face until he jerked away. Reverberating through the house was the sound of Mrs. Skylar's fierce grief. She had lost a husband five years before to the mountains, and it seemed cruel to have her eldest son claimed as well.

"I let go," TJ said.

"You didn't let go."

"I held his hand; I told him I wouldn't let go, and then I just couldn't hang on."

"You did what you could."

"He was so heavy and my hands were so wet. I had taken off my gloves. I couldn't get a clean grip."

"It must have been horrible."

"It was worse than horrible. I killed my brother."

"Really, you didn't."

"She thinks so," he said, jerking his head toward the servant's staircase leading up to the second floor. "She told me to get out. Get out and never come back."

"She doesn't mean it. She's a mother who's lost a son."

He jerked away from the embrace she extended to comfort him.

"TJ, it helps to talk about it."

"No, Paige, it doesn't help to talk. I could talk and talk until all the words were used up. But it doesn't change what happened out there on the mountain. And she knows it." He jabbed his finger in the direction of the stairs. "And so does everyone else."

"TJ, please. No one could possibly blame . . ."

But he was already charging through the dining room, shouldering past the gas station owner and his wife, mumbling a barely civil *excuse me* to the mayor, and then—gone. The exhaust of his pickup left a dark sooty mark on the virgin snow.

He hadn't returned for the wake that had brought the Sugar Mountain residents together in shock and sorrow. When he didn't return for the funeral, his absence was widely commented upon as his two younger brothers took their mother up to the first pew of Faith Union. They had been on the mountain, it was remembered, and were acting now like twin pillars to hold up their grieving mother.

TJ? Most agreed in side whispers and knowing looks that he had tried his best and it must have been hellish in the moment of failure. Naturally there were some who said that TJ could have done better, could have done more. He had guided on the mountains near Vail and Aspen. All the Skylar brothers were nimble and strong on the mountains—but TJ had always been known as the best of them.

But now, not even here for his family when they needed him!

Paige worried for TJ, even as she grieved for Jack. After the funeral, she drove to the roadhouse bar that nice ladies didn't frequent. Couldn't find him. Went to the mayor's neighborhood tavern decorated with reproachfully cheery lights. She went out to the valley set beneath the Sugar Mountain peaks. A yellow flickering plastic ribbon marked out where Jack's body had fallen.

But there was no sign of TJ.

She heard steps on the staircase outside and wondered if it were her mother . . . again.

She opened the door to the dark, star-laden night.

TJ stepped up the last stair and towered over her. He looked weary and beaten. His forehead had a thin crease of red where he had been hurt. He wore jeans, a flannel work shirt, a down vest, and hiking boots.

She threw her arms around him, crying out, "TJ, I was so damned worried about you."

He hesitated, and for a moment all she had in her arms was a down vest. But then, tentatively, he accepted her hug. And his body shuddered with a sob. She pulled him into the apartment, slamming the door shut on the cold, dry air. She kissed his tears until his cheeks were dry.

And then they both became uncomfortably aware.

"Baby, don't kiss me like that," he said huskily. "I've been to hell and back and I'm weak and I'm weary."

"I know what I'm doing," Paige lied.

"Like hell," he said and jerked out of her arms. "I shouldn't have come here."

"No! You should be here. I . . ."

Something, some warning glint in his eye, stopped her from saying what she meant. That she loved him. That she'd always loved him, that there had never been a day she hadn't known it, even when she was just a first grader and he sat at the desk across the aisle.

She didn't say it. She had spent a lifetime not saying it.

"I'm not able to talk."

"I'm not asking you to," she said, suddenly possessed of a feminine wisdom. He could not talk. He could not cry. He could not put away his manliness to get in touch with feelings. He needed something uniquely masculine. He needed sexual healing, even if he could never, ever recognize his own weakness and dependency on her.

She kissed him, uncertain at first, but she was not completely without experience. Strong full lips met hers, at first held in check, then opening to possess hers. She put her hand through the unzipped vest to where the smooth, warm flannel stretched over hard muscle.

He pulled away abruptly and said in a ragged voice, "I'm the adult here. We shouldn't be . . ."

She put a finger on his lips.

"I'm eighteen. I can drive, vote, and join the Army. I'll be the adult tonight."

"But I'm not the kind of man . . ."

"I know what kind of man you are."

"I can't even think about a relationship."

"I'm not looking for a relationship," she said. "I'm not looking for a morning after. I'm looking for tonight. Because I guess we're both figuring out that every day might not have a tomorrow to it."

He regarded her speculatively. And then picked her up and carried her into the next room, to the canopied bed.

The next morning, she got up and did the most unselfish thing she knew how to do.

"That was nice," she said, rising from the bed and pulling on a pair of jeans. She was grateful that she had not bled. That there was no way he could have known, because to know would have added to the weight on his shoulders.

She slapped him on his naked butt as if he were a good horse gone lazy. The pained look on his face might have been mistaken for a physical reaction. But Paige was not fooled. He looked at her, blinking twice, and then shame took over.

"That was a thank-you," she said with a great deal of bravado. "Let's not do that again, okay? Wouldn't want to ruin a good friendship."

He lifted his head from the pillow and opened his mouth as if he would argue with her.

"I'd rather be your friend in ten years than your ex-girlfriend," Paige pointed out.

He closed his mouth, jogged his Adam's apple as he swallowed, thinking through the implications of what she was suggesting.

"I'm so sorry," he said. "I took advant—"

"I'm not sorry," Paige said. "It was what both of us needed. No regrets, TJ. No regrets."

She buttoned her blouse up to her collarbone. She realized he wasn't persuaded.

He turned over on his back. His chest was massive, powerfully defined, its smoothness marred only by a line of hair that ran between his pectorals, down to his belly and from there, under the flannel sheets to . . .

She could not help but gaze.

"Paige, I . . . I love you. I really do."

She bit her lip against the pain caused by his declaration. How many times she had hoped that he would turn to her with just such words! But they were not said without guilt, shame, and a crushing sense of responsibility.

"You know darned well you don't have a monogamous bone in your body," she said, springing from the bed and beelining for the door. "TJ Skylar, I'm far too good a friend for you to waste on love."

"How do you even know that men and women can be friends?" he called out after her.

"I guess we have the rest of our lives to find out if they can," Paige said . . . and shut the door on him. On that part of her life. When he knocked on her parents' back door an hour later, he was freshly shaved and he told her he was going back to school early. It was only with great effort that he met her eyes, but she shushed him when he tried to say more, as she would do many times during the coming semester, until at last he believed what she told him. That this was a onetime thing—a mistake, but not a fatal one; that friendship was much more enduring and truly her only wish.

"No regrets," she told him many times. "No regrets, TJ."

Until she herself was persuaded.

SIX

"Sure there's a bus," the desk clerk said, looking up from his newspaper. "It'll be here tomorrow morning. First thing. But it doesn't go to New York. Gets into our nation's capital by, oh, by Wednesday night. Gotta lot of stops, you know. You could go to Washington and then catch a train."

"Okay, okay. There's no bus today heading for New York?"

The desk clerk stared reproachfully, as if the notion of a bus invading this stretch of road more often than every other day was ungodly wastefulness.

"Every other day to Washington, D.C. Just like clockwork."

A very slow clock, TJ thought.

"Airport?"

"Lancaster Airport's been closed on account of the storm."

"How about a limousine service?"

The desk clerk smiled indulgently.

"Don't have them big cars 'round here."

"Cabs?"

The clerk leaned his chair back on two legs and slipped back the lace curtains.

"That's what folks around here would call a cab," he said, arching his chin through the fabric to the road.

TJ stared.

Clip-clop. Clip-clop-clop. Clip-clop. A black buggy with a bright-orange triangle clipped to its back window. Alongside it skipped three children—two boys with broad black-brimmed hats and somber suits and a girl who wore a dark gray dress which skimmed her ankles. Her hair and the expression on her face was covered by a white lace bonnet. He felt he had been transported back into another century.

"What the—"

"Amish," the desk clerk explained. "Five miles an hour in those buggies. And five miles an hour if you're driving a car behind one of them things. Too bad it's not Sunday, you could hitch a ride back to New York."

"Sunday?"

"Everything in Lancaster is closed on Sundays. Plenty of you all come out here on weekends to get a little taste of the simple life. Buy a quilt, a can of preserves, a piece of furniture. One of them Amish guys serves dinner in his house—New Yorkers pay twenty bucks a head to eat plain, home-cooked food that I could just as well give 'em. Meat and three sides—that's what draws them here. Simple life. All that quaintness wrapped up in a weekend holiday. And then on Sunday, the modern people all clear out. Had enough simplicity."

"I can't wait until Sunday."

"Buddy, if you don't make peace with that woman

of yours, you ain't getting out of Lancaster County until you find yourself a New Yorker with an extra seat in his car and kindness in his heart."

TJ looked out at the parking lot. Her car was still sitting in the space in front of cabin six.

"We're going in opposite directions," TJ said.

"All young lovers think that at times."

TJ pulled his wallet out. Counted the Ben Franklins, the Andrew Jacksons, the Abraham Lincolns.

"I'll pay you two hundred dollars to drive me to New York. An extra fifty if we get to my office by two o'clock."

The desk clerk leaned over the desk and flipped the closed/open sign on the door.

"I've always wanted to see the Statue of Liberty."

Paige adjusted the rearview mirror and watched TJ stride out of the Get Some Sleep Inn office. Behind him strolled the desk clerk, who put down TJ's briefcase and weekender so he could lock the office door. He kicked the vending machine, and a soda can rolled out into his hand. Then he hoisted the bags into the trunk of a shell-pink boat of a car and popped open his drink.

TJ walked across the parking lot and shoved his head into the passenger-side window of her car.

"Are you going to be all right?"

"Of course I will be," Paige lied, adding in complete truthfulness, "I'm sorry about kidnapping you. I thought it would work; I thought I could bring you to your senses. In fact, I thought after you got over being mad at me, we'd have a fun road trip and spend some time reevaluating our lives."

His lips drew together in a thin, disapproving line. There wasn't going to be any reevaluating of his life.

"Don't ever try this on anyone else. They might not forgive you."

"And I'm sorry about bringing up . . ."

The look he gave her stopped her midsentence.

Jack was off-limits. Always off-limits.

She wondered what she would tell his mom.

"Call if you need anything," TJ said. "I'll be in Chicago in two days. I think I'm staying at the Palmer House Hotel; but if you can't reach me there, you can get me through my office. If you need money, a place to stay, even just someone to talk to. The usuals."

The usuals of their friendship.

"I can take care of myself."

He regarded her speculatively.

"Have you got enough money?"

"Five hundred in cash. Some traveler's checks and my credit cards."

"Maps?"

She nodded at the glove compartment.

"I know where I'm going. Interstate 70 all the way. Besides, I've done this before."

Four times a year she had gone back during college, borrowing TJ's car. Later, when she had money but not the time, she flew in once a year to see Teddy, to see her parents and endure the have-you-met-any-nice-men-in-New York interrogation.

"Call," he said.

"I will."

"Have a good time."

"I intend to."

"Find what you're looking for."

"I hope so."

"Well, goodbye," he said.

"Goodbye."

He patted her car affectionately and walked across the lot to the pink car. Suddenly, the car belched, rattled, and then roared to life with a frothy gray billow of exhaust. It backed out, its back fin nearly hitting her bumper. Then with a roar and a caching-caching of its muffler, the car breezed out of the parking lot. It turned east, toward New York.

"Goodbye, TJ," she said.

Paige turned the ignition. She had done everything she could. She could do no more. She could no longer bear the boxed-in, pressure-cooker life of a New York professional. He could not walk away from it. She wanted a family—a husband and children all her own. Although she wasn't sure where she would find it, she knew she couldn't find that in New York, when every man was a second best to TJ.

She backed out slowly and waited at the stop sign for a black horse-drawn carriage to pass as slowly as a funeral procession.

Her passenger door opened. A weekender bag flew past her shoulder to the backseat, followed by a briefcase. TJ slumped into the seat.

"Chicago," TJ said, without looking at her. "You can drop me off in Chicago."

"What changed your mind?"

"The Amish."

"Really? They made you think about your life and where it's going?"

"They didn't make me think anything. They go five miles an hour and you're not allowed to pass them. I could walk to New York faster than that man could get me there. We were stuck behind a buggy and four cows."

"But I'm not going to New York."

"You weren't listening. I have to turn around and fly out to Chicago the minute I get back to New York. You can get me to Chicago by midnight, right?"

"I'd have to take a detour at Indianapolis up Route 65," Paige agreed, suppressing a smile. Logistics, huh? "I can get you to Chicago."

"One thing, Paige."

"What?"

"You are not to use this as an opportunity to change my mind."

"The very idea!" she exclaimed, touching her finger to her breast bone in an expression of outrage.

"And could you put your blouse back on?" he asked, reaching into the backseat. "It would make me feel a lot better."

"Okay, but when it gets hot I'm taking it off."

At one o'clock, they stopped thirty miles past Bedford for lunch at a diner tucked away off the highway. When they returned to the car, Paige thought she noticed something odd about the engine turning. But she didn't say anything. Nonetheless, five hundred yards down the road leading back to the highway, she pressed her foot on the accelerator and the familiar charge didn't come. The engine sput-sput-sputtered to a halt in front of a field of wheat.

"Are we out of gas?" TJ asked.

"It says I have a quarter-tank."

"Then what's the matter?"

"I don't know."

"What's the matter?" TJ repeated three hours later. The mechanic wiped his oil-covered hands on the front of his coverall. He ducked his head and smiled good-naturedly though TJ had asked the same question every five minutes since the tow into Herman's Gas and Automotive Services. Herman had grunted, growled, moaned, and shrugged in reply—never lifting his head out from under the hood of Paige's little sports car.

But this time he patted the hood shut with all the affection and pride of a parent.

"Oh, not much wrong, just this little gadget right here," he said in an accent thick with the German that was his first language. His stubby hand opened to display a slender, delicate piece of copper.

"Fix it," TJ said.

"Can't do that." The owner and sole employee of Herman's Gas and Automotives shook his head mournfully. "It's broken clear through."

"Replace it."

"*Ja*, I can do that," Herman nodded. "I'll order the piece as soon as you get off my phone."

Herman wiped his sweaty, shiny head with a handkerchief and put on a SunOil baseball cap he pulled out of his back pocket.

"My phone, young man."

TJ looked down at the receiver he held in his hand. "I'll have to get back to you," he told his caller.

"Danke shoen," Herman said. Receiver in hand, he followed the long, twirling cord around the tool cart, over the flatbed of a customer's pickup, and through a narrow cement hallway to the office. "Soon as I track down this itsy-bitsy little part, mister, we'll have you and your lady on your way."

At the desk, Paige looked up from her tabloid magazine and her strawberry licorice. The money she owed Herman for her snacks was stacked beside the cash register.

Her silk blouse was a puddle on the vinyl chair by the window. TJ picked it up and shoved it in his back pocket. He didn't like her not wearing her blouse. Made for a pink sunburn on her shoulders. Didn't she realize the danger of skin cancer?

"Did you know that Michael Jackson got married to Elvis Presley's daughter?" Paige asked. "You learn so much when you read a weekly paper."

Herman laughed loudly. "That's old news." He pulled a well-used yellow pages from a shelf behind her head. "He got divorced from her and then he married Debbie Rowe, his plastic surgeon's office assistant; and they had a son, Prince, and then a daughter Paris. And now they're divorced because he's . . ."

"Can we just order the part?" TJ interrupted.

Paige and Herman looked at him. Disapproval on both counts. This was interesting stuff to talk about.

"Yes, sir, Mr. Skylar, I'll hop right to it."

Paige pushed her magazine and candies to one side of the desk and stood up to give room to Herman.

"You don't have to be a jerk, TJ," she said. "He's doing the best he can."

"I know he is. He's just . . ." He looked at Herman.

"*Ja,* I'm slow." Herman completed TJ's thought. "But I get the job done."

"TJ, not everyone runs on New York time."

"You're just as efficient as I am."

"Not anymore. I'm trading quality time for quantity time." She flopped down on a green vinyl couch by the window. Her shiny hair fanned out behind her head like a glowing crown. She bit on a licorice stick. Her lips were stained strawberry pink. TJ looked away.

"That's because you only have to make it to Colorado by Friday night. Me, every minute I waste out here in the middle of nowhere . . ."

"Pennsylvania," Herman corrected, ducking his head quickly when he caught TJ's don't-go-there look.

"All right, Pennsylvania. But every minute I'm not in the office I'm losing money."

"I don't know when you stopped caring about anything that doesn't have a price tag," Paige murmured.

"Enough!" Herman said. "I cannot hear myself think with you two talking like this. I need silence to do my work."

He hunched over the yellow pages.

Paige scooted nearer to the armrest so that TJ could slump on the green vinyl couch.

Herman called a parts shop just fifty miles away. Another that was near Uniontown. Another that was recommended by the shop near Uniontown.

"Earliest I can have the part in is day after tomorrow," he said after six more calls. "It'll still take me a day to install. Foreign car, you know. But a real beauty. I love just having a chance to touch it, to be with it. Such an angel of a car."

TJ put his head in his hands.

"Look, Herman, I'm glad you feel this way about your work, but I've gotta be in Chicago by—"

The phone rang.

Herman picked it up.

"Herman's Gas and Automo—*ja,* he's here."

He handed the phone to TJ and let him have the desk chair.

"Herman, I've got a business proposal for you," Paige said.

Herman's eyes, as small and dark as raisins, darted toward TJ.

"Let's talk . . . out in the parking lot," Paige suggested.

Herman and Paige walked out onto the blacktop. Over the phone, TJ's secretary read to him the closing numbers from the New York Stock Exchange. TJ craned his neck to watch Paige and the gorilla-sized mechanic. Herman shook his head at something Paige said, but at least he wasn't gawking. Poor Paige didn't realize she was playing with fire because most men would . . . TJ stood up—Paige touched Herman's shoulder, spoke again, nodded vigorously.

"TJ, are you listening to me?" his secretary demanded.

"Yeah, yeah, I'm listening."

Again, Herman shook his head. TJ gnawed at a twizzler. He didn't like the idea of her touching Herman. It was worse because she was wearing that tiny top. Why had she had to take off the silk blouse just because it had gotten stained with oil when they both stuck their heads under the hood of the car? And then there were those jeans. Paige turned away from the picture window, displaying buttocks that were round and full and . . .

"TJ, did you hear me?" his secretary interrupted.

"Yeah, sure I did."

"So . . . do you want to buy or sell?"

He stood up so he could get a better look over the magazine display rack. When she shifted her weight from one leg to another it made her hips jut out. Herman looked around her, getting a gander at the curves no doubt. Then Herman picked up a candy wrapper from the ground—the gas station was impeccably clean. TJ wondered if her waist were small enough to put his hands around. Looked like it. He hadn't ever noticed her waist before, at least not that he could remember.

"I just want to protect her," he said aloud. "It's not like I want to do anything."

"TJ, you are not making any sense."

"Oh, yeah, go ahead," he said, sitting down. He scrunched his head down onto his shoulders so that he couldn't be distracted. "You were telling me about Intel stock."

"Down two and five-eighths."

"And what about SunOil?"

"Up four and a quarter. Rumors of the deal are hitting the street. By the way, Shawna called and said she'd meet you in Chicago. Palmer House Hotel. You are going to make it to Chicago, aren't you?"

Shawna. He reached into his jeans pocket and pulled out a tiny blue velvet box. Flipping the lid, he stared morosely at the fiery five-carat square-cut diamond set in platinum.

It wasn't that he'd asked. It wasn't that she'd asked. But it was one of those things he knew he should do. She really was intelligent, much more so than anybody ever guessed. And she had suggested that there came a time in a man's life . . . and that they'd make a great team.

A provocative picture caught his eye. Pinned up on the inside of a steel locker door behind the desk was a SunOil calendar. Herman hadn't caught up to June. Or even May. No, Herman had left the calendar on April, undoubtedly the cruelest month—Shawna with her trademark chiclet teeth and casually blow-dried curls (which took a stylist three hours and a gallon of gel), naked from the waist up (at least as far as anyone who didn't know she used a body-stocking could tell). Two cans of SunOil windshield wiper fluid were held strategically in place by slim, manicured fingers.

He kicked the steel locker door shut.

Then, feeling guilty about how he was treating his future bride, he opened the steel locker. Ripped away April, May, June. July was a month Shawna was particularly proud of. She wore tight mechanic's coveralls and held up a SunOil oil filter. But she was pretty much decent. Except for the come-here-you-savage expression.

"I'll get to Chicago as soon as I can. Call and tell 'em I'm running late."

He heard laughter outside. He stood up.

Herman wiped his chunky hands on a delicate white handkerchief he produced from a back pocket. Only after he had buffed his hands to a baby light pink did he take Paige's outstretched hand. He kissed the tips of her index and middle fingers.

TJ was outraged. This was what happened when Paige started acting like what she wasn't, which is to say, a bit of a wild woman. He had to protect her.

"Gotta go," he said. "Call you later."

"Later, I'm going home," his secretary reminded him. "Do you understand that I have a personal life?"

TJ slammed down the phone and headed outside.

"All right, what the hell is—"

"We have a car," Paige said.

"Yeah, but why does he have to kiss your . . . we do?"

"We do now. Herman's car. And I'll drive you straight to Chicago."

He thought of Shawna.

"We can wait to get the part fixed," he said.

"No, no, that's okay, TJ. I know how much it means to you to get to Chicago. We'll go right after dinner. At Herman's house."

Herman's mouth opened in a hideously friendly

grin. A perfect gold cap on his left canine tooth twinkled in the setting sun. TJ didn't like the idea of this man kissing Paige's hand.

"Aren't most business deals sealed with a handshake?" he asked irritably.

"Not when one of the parties to the deal is so lovely," Herman said.

"TJ, get a grip on yourself," Paige hissed. "This man is giving us a car."

"My sister Berte makes beef-liver dumplings that will make you swoon," Herman said, seeming not to notice TJ's scowl. "And it would be our pleasure to be your host for a meal before you continue your journey."

"Besides, we have to drive Herman home when we pick up the car," Paige said. "It's his car."

"We're getting the car from Herman's house?"

Herman beamed.

"An even trade," Paige explained. "My car for his."

TJ's mouth opened, words forming and dissolving on his tongue.

"It's a 1967 Mustang convertible," Herman said, chest and stomach straining against his coveralls as he rose in stature. "I rebuilt the engine myself."

"Paige, you can't trade in your car for a Mustang. Do you have any idea how much money you're losing?"

Paige shrugged. TJ poked his finger at Herman's chest.

"You're taking advantage of this woman."

Herman crossed his arms. He wasn't as tall as TJ,

wasn't exploding with outrage like TJ, and he didn't even have a full head of hair. But Herman didn't back down. Or maybe it was just that Herman didn't know enough to be intimidated.

"She's the one who proposed the deal."

"Do you have any idea how much her car costs?" Herman nodded.

"*Ja*, it's a beauty. I could never in my life afford such a treasure of a car. But your woman is still getting the better deal."

"Oh, really?"

"*Ja*, because my car runs."

SEVEN

"I can't believe you gave up your car," TJ said when he squeezed next to Paige in the tow truck. "That car was your pride and joy. You saved three years for it."

Paige shrugged. The freckles on her shoulders brightened.

"Why don't you just tell him you'll pick up your car on the way back from Sugar Mountain?"

"Because I'm not coming back."

TJ's mouth went dry.

"What do you mean, *not coming back?*"

Paige appeared to take great interest in the vista beyond the truck's windshield. Herman locking up the gas station office. Herman pinching the dead-heads from the geraniums planted in a kettle drum beside the office door. Herman patting the pockets of his coveralls until he remembered that he had left the keys to the tow truck in the ignition.

"Paige, what does *not coming back* mean?"

"It means *not coming back.*"

"Not coming back to New York at all?"

Paige looked very much as she had when she had whacked the baseball through the Skylar living room window. Just as she had done then, she swallowed hard, dropped her eyes, and then found a reservoir of gumption. She tilted her chin high and challenged him with her eyes. This time there wasn't as much guilt as when she had slugged the baseball.

"I quit my job."

"No, Paige, tell me you didn't."

"I did."

"Did you tell Walter Greenough about this?"

"Yes, two weeks ago."

"And you didn't tell me?"

"No, I didn't. I knew you'd try to talk me out of it."

"Damn right I would," he said, slamming his fist on the dashboard. "But, Paige, we always talk about our plans with each other."

"I'll talk to you about it now."

"But why not two weeks ago?"

"TJ, haven't you ever made a decision without consulting me?"

He thought about Shawna. That wasn't really a decision. That was more like an inevitable.

"Minor things, yes. But we've always talked about your job. What'd Walter say?"

"Walter said that my health benefits run for another year. That I'd be missed. And that I could come back anytime."

"Good. Anytime sounds like right after the weekend. Didn't it ever dawn on you that you don't have to quit your job to go to your high school reunion?"

"TJ, you're not taking me seriously."

"You've kidnapped me; you threw away my cell phone; I'm stuck in the wilderness of Pennsylvania when I'm supposed to be taking care of business. It's hard to take you seriously. I'll call Greenough tonight and tell him that you'll be coming back."

"You'll do no such thing."

"Paige, I've always taken care of—"

"You've always taken care of me. I know. But I'm not your little sister. I'm not your junior. I'm not your sidekick. You're not running my life."

"I never wanted to."

"I will drive you to Chicago if you want. But you are not to interfere with or make fun of my plans. In fact, I don't want you opening your mouth at all for the entire ride."

"And if I open my mouth?"

Herman opened the driver's side door and hoisted himself onto the seat.

"You can stay with Herman if you don't want to drive with me," Paige said.

On hearing his name, Herman leaned forward, grinning at TJ.

"You'd be welcome," he said. And he turned the key in the ignition. The engine rev was accompanied by flirty, feisty polka music from the radio. Herman knew all the words to the tune and repeated each chorus with fierce abandon.

Paige looked at TJ and drew her finger across her mouth with a twisting jerk of her wrist that indicated a key locking a door and then a more graceful fluttering of her fingers indicating the key was to be thrown away.

Not a word, she said silently. *Not a single word.*

* * *

To her brother Herman's applause, Berte brought a creamy porcelain soup tureen from the kitchen. She placed it on a silver trivet in the middle of the ocean of lace and platters and trays that was the dining room table.

"My little dumplings," she said, raising the lid to allow the aromas to tantalize her guests.

Berte was built of the same proportions as her brother. But where Herman embodied masculine coarseness, visible even under the white shirt and tie into which he had changed for supper, Berte's girth was softly feminine. No anorexic supermodel, no sculpted Hollywood femme, she was a beauty of a different sort, a different age.

It was not inconceivable that Reubens himself would have courted her. For her beauty, delicately enriched with a pale blue silk dress—and for her cooking.

Three courses had come to the table in advance of the celebrated dumplings. There was a potato salad which put to shame all the New York deli offerings Paige and TJ had ever praised. Followed by sugared beets that melted in one's mouth—and left a purple stain on the tongue that only a gulp of elderberry wine and a bite of homemade onion bread could erase.

While TJ sat mute, there was only one subject considered worthy of attention at Herman and Berte's table. The food. Food was to be marveled at, sighed over, savored at length. Each course was compared and contrasted with offerings that Berte had made for church socials, bridge club pot lucks, and Christmas Eves past. Which led to reminiscences of other feasts made by other, less talented but no less loved, cooks. This discussion, led by Herman, was punctuated by lavish praise from Paige, praise that made Berte blush.

Then Herman and Berte would politely pose a question concerning the food to be found in New York. Paige's answer would be greeted by Berte's clucking in sympathy and a grunt of concern from Herman.

New Yorkers, the brother and sister concluded, were a sorry, deprived lot. Grabbing a meal from a fast-food joint or from one of the thousands of street vendors was a hardship they themselves could not have borne.

And when Paige told about trendy restaurants, themed or unthemed, they complained mightily that no one should have to pay such prices.

The good Lord gave man food to be enjoyed, Herman declared. It was one of the finest pleasures in life, second only to marriage and children.

Paige nodded, staring all the while at TJ.

The good Lord didn't mention profit-taking, corner offices, or stress-related ulcers, she said with just the briefest narrowing of her eyes.

TJ was a bolter—used to eating quickly to satisfy gnawing hungers while on the run. He ate knishes from sidewalk vendors, chowed on hot dogs as he strode city streets, and had his secretary order up from the deli when he couldn't get away from the office. Food was fuel. Except, of course, for client dinners—and those were inefficient means of dealing in business, but must be endured.

This? Oh, this was a total time-waster.

He suffered from only slightly less anxiety than he had during the day because Paige had finally taken off that ridiculously brazen tank top.

She had changed into a pale pink dress that covered everything from her collarbone to her ankles. A ruffle here. A dainty button there. A delicate rosette of satin at the elbow.

Covered from head to toe. But still discombobulating because this wasn't a businesswoman's kind of dress, wasn't a hanging-out-with-the-buddies-to-watch-Monday-night-football dress, and he wasn't given the distraction of a TJ-hungry hottie in a tight dress.

In fact, if anything, all that covering up made him more aware of her femininity. Aware and confused. Very confused.

Blame it on Herman. Herman required everyone to change for dinner. Insisted on holding his sister's chair for her. And insisted that TJ hold Paige's. Stood up when either woman entered or left the room. Insisted that TJ do the same—until TJ felt that he was a marionette.

He asked Berte if Herman were always like this.

"How would he be different?" she asked, puzzled.

The dress; Herman's Old World manners; Paige's hair, which was not sleekly blow-dried but was a mass of curls and waves; the delicate pink of her lips—all of these factors made TJ more aware of the fact that Paige was a woman and TJ was a man.

It was an oddly uncomfortable fact to discover this so late in life.

TJ ate three bites during each of the first three courses; and when he saw the tureen filled with beef broth and brown, bulging dumplings, he shook his head.

"Not hungry," he said.

Berte looked crestfallen.

"Vegetarian," he explained.

"You're not a vegetarian," Paige corrected.

He grimaced.

"No offense, Herman, but my watch says nine; and if we start now, it's still going to take until dawn to reach Chicago."

"You're not going to start such a long drive now!" Berte declared.

"I don't think it's such a good idea either," Paige said. "I'm kinda tired."

She yawned delicately behind her hand.

"Besides, I've finished a glass of wine and it's not wise to drive after drinking."

"Ja," Berte agreed, pouring wine into TJ's glass.

"I'll drive," TJ said, getting up. "Great dinner, but we really should head out."

"No," Herman said stolidly. "You don't leave."

TJ squared his shoulders. He'd had quite enough of Herman.

"And why not?"

"Because I have the car keys. Madam," he said, addressing Paige, "do you wish me to give him the car keys?"

"Absolutely not. TJ, sit down. You're going to finish dinner first. Then we'll drive. Maybe."

Chastened, disheartened, defeated, he sat down. Berte ladled broth and dumplings into his bowl.

"TJ, why don't you tell Herman and Berte about

that dinner you gave for the president of Motorcon? It was Thai food, wasn't it?"

Actually, TJ could remember nothing of the dinner party two months before except the fifty-million-dollar buyout he had negotiated over coffee. He counted it as a working dinner—and, therefore, had only given the barest nod to the food placed in front of him. The Motorcon executives had figured out over appetizers that Motorcon would become a subsidiary of SunOil, with SunOil's handpicked team filling its key positions.

The Thai food was expensive, opulent, and very trendy. But it could have been cardboard for all it mattered.

But three people looked expectantly at him.

"Uh, they had . . . you know, food."

His words hung over the table. Herman nodded sagely. Berte looked blankly puzzled. And Paige stared heavenward. Okay, he'd try again when what he'd really like to say was, "Paige, there's a velvet box in my pocket that I know that I really should give to Shawna and I have to be in Chicago for the biggest deal of my life and you're really confusing the heck out of me because you're taking our friendship and changing it."

"There were these little things." He made a small cube with his fingers. "Vegetable things. We had those before dinner."

"I see," Herman said. "Who exactly was at this dinner?"

"The Motorcon team." TJ shrugged. "President, Finance Officer, Vice Presidents of Sales and Employee Relations."

"You are friends with all these people?"

"Oh, no, not at all. I was negotiating the purchase of their company."

"Ah, Motorcon's funeral," Herman said sagely.

"Some funeral. The company got fifty million dollars. And after it's distributed among their shareholders, the president and his executives will each receive a million a piece. And none of them will ever have to work another day in their lives."

"Can they get jobs elsewhere?" Berte asked.

"Well, no, because part of the noncompetition clause with SunOil is that they don't work in the industry again," TJ said, warming to this topic. "It's very common in buyouts. You don't want them turning around and opening up a competing company."

"Funeral," Herman repeated.

"Taking away a man's work is the same as taking away his reason for being," Berte said.

"But it's not like that. If after SunOil bought Motorcon these guys turned around and started another business they'd beat SunOil to a pulp in the marketplace. In fact, that's why SunOil has to buy out Motorcon. These guys are too good at what they do. And since both companies are getting hit hard by the industry, they have to pool resources. One executive team has to go."

"That's a waste of talent. And talent is the biggest resource those companies have."

"Funny. That's what Shawna says."

"Shawna is the Oil-Me-Up Girl," Paige said.

Berte looked shocked at mention of Shawna's name at the table. Herman's jowls shook.

"I wouldn't know her," he said firmly.

A dessert of apple turnovers with ice cream and

cheddar cheese wedges was served, and the ambition to drive to Chicago faltered. A glass of elderberry wine was poured for TJ. And when he toasted his hosts, his eyes met those of the friend he was soon to part with. Paige was his buddy, his pal, his occasional tennis partner, the sister he had never had.

He'd miss her, he thought. Because if she weren't in the city, weren't part of the action, he knew they wouldn't connect in the same way. She was going on a journey far beyond a simple weekend catching up with high school classmates faintly remembered.

He lifted his glass in an across-the-table salute. He didn't like it, but he'd have to wish her well.

The velvet jewel box burning a hole in his pocket was forgotten. He had not asked Shawna to marry him. Shawna hadn't asked him.

Maybe he wasn't marrying the Oil-Me-Up Girl at all.

He was going to remain a New York single male with a straight-up ambition to succeed. After all, there weren't too many of his kind. He had thought Paige was one of them, but it turned out she was a woman.

And she was leaving.

EIGHT

After dinner, Herman announced that it was time for bed. Berte said that she had laid new linens on the guest room bed. TJ stood up from the table and was prepared to argue the matter of driving straight through to Chicago.

But he felt the light-headedness of two glasses of wine and realized it would be foolish, to say nothing of dangerous, to drive.

"You two will be comfortable in the guest room," Berte said.

"We won't be sleeping together," Paige said.

"But you are married, no?" Berte asked.

"No, we're not."

Berte's mouth opened in a small round O.

"Engaged, then?"

"No."

Herman cocked an eyebrow.

"Significant?"

"We're friends."

Berte and Herman exchanged a mirthful glance.

"Men and women can't be friends," Berte pointed out. "Men will always want more."

"Women can sometimes want more," Herman suggested.

"But one or the other always wants more," Berte concluded.

"We've been friends for a long time," Paige said. "It's not like that. TJ doesn't have the slightest interest in me, and I don't have any in him."

Why did those words make TJ so uncomfortable? Must be indigestion from all those dumplings.

"Yeah, we have the perfect friendship," he said.

"We're really friends," Paige said.

Berte shook her head at the notion.

Herman smirked.

Berte opened a neatly organized linen closet and produced a blanket and two pillows for TJ.

"You'll be comfortable on the couch," she told him.

TJ looked at Paige.

Why do you always get the bed? he asked silently.

She shrugged prettily.

Contrary to Berte's assertion, he was not at all comfortable.

Herman and Berte's couch was not a pleasure given to man by the good Lord—like hearty food, good wine, and Pennsylvania farmland. In fact, it wasn't a pleasure at all.

The couch was torture, from the tufted peaks and valleys of the tweedy upholstery to the springs beneath the scratchy fabric which coiled and roiled against his muscles. He touched the luminator dial on his watch. A half hour spent tossing and turning. He'd be a wreck on the road if he tried driving without a good night's sleep.

A thousand possible car catastrophes tripped through his semiconsciousness. All of them involved falling asleep at the wheel, and all made him sit up straight before remembering that a couch was a couch and the car was in Herman's garage.

He closed his eyes and counted sheep. But the sheep frolicked and danced like characters in a Looney Toons cartoon.

He tried something he had used in college—thinking of celebrities whose first and last names began with the same letter. Alan Alda. Babs Branson. No, she wasn't really a celebrity. She was his neighbor. B. B. Somebody with a first and last name beginning with B. Barbra Streisand. No, Streisand starts with S. But Streisand made him think of Shawna.

How was he going to deal with Shawna? She thought marriage was a good idea. It probably was, from a marketing perspective and maybe even a personal one. Sometimes he thought he was handicapped in the relationship department. He dated, oh, sure. He got lucky, to use the language of the locker room. But he didn't connect. Not in any real way.

Except, of course, with Paige. But that was precisely because he didn't have any romantic expectations. What was he going to do with her gone? He rolled over on his back, wondering if the box springs in the couch were going to permanently damage his kidneys.

He was one year older than Paige—the Sugar Mountain elementary school principal firmly believed in holding back boys one year before kindergarten. Gave them extra maturity, so they could be equal to the girls who developed faster. So he was twenty-nine to Paige's twenty-eight. Twenty-nine was not old for a bachelor. In fact, he'd have to be five or six years older before anyone in his circle of acquaintances and colleagues would question his single status. Before rumors of being commitment-phobic, immature, or gay would come up.

He was happy being a bachelor. His time was his own—at least the time he wasn't working, which was, oh, at least forty-five minutes a day. He could drink straight out of the milk carton—of course, the milk, if there were milk in the refrigerator, was almost always sour because he never got around to shopping. He could date any woman he wanted—which he did, two or three times, before he had to endure the where-is-this-relationship-heading talk. He didn't have to deal with noisy children, nosy in-laws, being in the doghouse for missing an anniversary . . . or having a beautiful woman kiss him hello every day when he got home from the office.

He rolled over on his stomach. Put the pillow over his head. Felt a stabbing sensation in his stomach which, no doubt, was food poisoning from Berte's cooking . . . but on investigation turned out to be a needle attached to an embroidery project.

Outside, a church bell rang two times.

New York was always noisy, with neighbors playing music, cabs honking, ambulances squealing, jackhammers drilling; and he had always fallen asleep in spite of being annoyed and disturbed. Now—nothing. Save the not-so-gentle snores of his hosts in bedrooms behind closed doors on opposite sides of the living room.

He got up, dragging his blanket behind him. He

felt his way through the kitchen to the guest bedroom. A thin thread of light glistened from beneath the door.

He knocked.

"Paige, open up."

A rustle of fabric, the tap of bare feet on a hardwood floor, and the door opened. He stared.

He wondered where the flannel pj's had gone.

Because she wasn't wearing any.

Instead, a gossamer-light nightgown and robe drifted over her curves and gathered at her slim ankles.

His mouth went dry.

"Uh."

"Yes?"

He noticed for the first time that she was wearing her reading glasses. She held up a paperback. He wondered if she were wearing panties. Something he had never wondered about.

"Uh, I can't sleep."

"Drink warm milk."

"I really can't sleep."

"Count sheep."

"They're too playful."

"What do you want from me?"

He glanced over her shoulder to the inviting sleigh bed. Hardwood with curves. A mattress that looked soft and forgiving. Pillows piled high, linens as white and unsullied as virgin snow.

"Please?"

She glowered.

"I don't think it's a good idea."

"Scout's honor. I won't do a thing."

"Fine."

She turned around and the sight of her rounded buttocks swish-swish-swishing against pale fabric made his boyish promise dry as dust.

"Wow. I mean, maybe I'd better take another try at the couch."

"Your choice," she said. And sat down on the bed, modestly arranging covers over her legs. "I'll be staying up to read for a while."

"Oh. Good. I mean, that's a very good idea. Commendable, your reading. People don't do enough of that these days. Reading is sort of a lost art. I'm thinking of reading that Tom Wolfe book right away. Except it's very big and that's intimidating."

She opened her book. Looked at him as if he were nuts.

He was babbling.

"Did I mention that functional illiteracy is a growing problem in the United States?"

The bed was sooo inviting, but Paige was like a five-alarm fireball that would burn him if he got close. He stepped inside the room, closing the door softly. He started to undo his jeans, but with one over-the-glasses look from Paige and a delicate clearing of her throat, he buttoned right up. He sat down on the very edge of the mattress, feeling the sweet surrender of real feathers. Ah, luxury. He lay down, pulled the covers up over his shoulders, and felt his entire body relax, his head caressed by a lavender-scented linen pillowcase.

Then he felt it.

A poke in his ribs.

"I didn't say you were sleeping on the bed," Paige said. "You can have that."

She pointed a slim finger at a dainty, chintz-covered chaise in the corner of the room. He looked at her once, hoping that he could communicate an entire why-can't-I argument in a glance, but she wasn't having any of that. She read her book.

He got up wearily.

Sat down wearily.

Looked at her wearily.

It was the kind of chaise upon which women spent rainy afternoons with a cup of tea and a romance novel. *Or their embroidery,* he thought sourly, pulling a needle and a long pink thread out from the seat. He put the needle on the dainty-as-a-salad-plate occasional table and tried to get comfy. He squirmed right, squirmed left. Dangled his ankles. Pulled his knees up to his chest. Put under those knees a pillow needlepointed with the words *Princess of Quite a Lot.* Glowered at Paige. Nearly whimpered.

She turned a page in her book, a book that must have been the most fascinating ever written, for she spared him not a glance, not a smidgen of pity.

Course, he'd never sleep. No, no, not with Paige right near him, her perfume as subtle as paper whites at Christmas and as potent as pheromones. Her naked flesh just two layers of sheer fabric away. When had she gotten so damn sexy?

Never get to sleep. And especially not while trying to pack a six-two, two-hundred-pound body on a piece of furniture that would be better used in a dollhouse.

No, no sleep. But he dutifully closed his eyes.

* * *

And then there was that woman. Again. She wore a gown of white satin. And a veil made out of the same material as Paige's nightgown. It completely covered her features.

She glided down the aisle as if she were on a gently moving conveyer belt. He had the vague sense that the people at SunOil were going to be mighty happy.

Out of the corner of his eye, he noticed the Motorcon executive team. They looked very somber. Herman was standing with them in a black suit. He scowled. Berte cried into a delicate handkerchief. Neither of them were offering best wishes or congratulations.

It wasn't a damn funeral; it was his wedding. His and . . . well, whatever-her-name-was.

He held out his hand to his new bride. He lifted her frothy veil. Surely the minister wouldn't mind, especially since he couldn't for the life of him remember when he had asked Shawna to marry him.

And one other thing.

Where was Paige? What kind of friend was she not to come to his funeral? Make that *wedding*.

NINE

Paige stepped over TJ on her way back from the tiny bathroom. Funny how he'd ended up on the floor. With his arms locked around the Princess-of-Quite-a-Lot pillow. One foot jammed under the nightstand. Peaceful look on his face, at least the side that wasn't squished into the rolls of the rag rug.

Odd sight, really. TJ at rest. Without a cell phone at his ear and a dozen highly profitable ideas orbiting his head.

She wondered if the women he bedded ever saw him like this.

Didn't matter, really.

None of her business.

Hadn't given it a thought since the day she put any romantic feelings for TJ in a little box.

Shouldn't get started now.

She shook his shoulder.

"TJ, wake up," she said.

Nothing.

"TJ."

Nothing.

"TJ, the Dow Jones industrial average lost four hundred points in the first hour of trading and the NASDAQ is off ten percent."

He jerked his head up, cracking his forehead against the bottom of the chintz chaise.

"What the—"

"Don't worry. New York markets aren't open yet. I'm sure American industry misses you terribly, but is still soldiering on without you."

He stared at her. Rubbed his eyes, scratched the stubble on his jaw. Stretched, bringing taut his knit, cotton polo shirt. He continued staring, eyeballing her as if she were the most unexpected vision.

She glanced down at her white t-shirt. It had sleeves that covered everything from the elbow up. A collar that didn't give away a thing. Really quite conservative, in its own way.

"We're not starting that stuff about my clothes again, are we?"

"No, it's just you were wearing white."

"I'm wearing white now."

"No, no, there was more."

"My nightgown?"

He rubbed his eyes again. And stared. Really stared.

Paige wasn't sure she liked the scrutiny.

"You were wearing white in my dream. Not a nightgown. Or a t-shirt. Was that you?"

Paige, couldn't resist. "What was I doing in your dream?" she pressed, curious.

He sat up. Looked at her with all the wonderment of a man seeing a touch of heaven in the female form. She thought she saw the word *wow* form on his lips. And without even touching her! His eyes widened and then he clamped his mouth shut. He crossed his arms over his chest.

"You were wearing a white jacket. A straitjacket. Because you're so damned crazy to drag me out here to the middle of nowhere."

She jerked to her feet.

"If you want to get to Chicago, you'd better get dressed. Five minutes, I'm rolling out of the driveway and not looking back."

"Okay," he said, stretching his back so that his body ran the length of the room. "But are you still giving it all up to chase some ridiculous notion of a simple life?"

"No, TJ. I realized that you're right and I'm wrong," she said irritably. She shoved her nightgown into her bag. "I can't quit my job. I would be an idiot if I did. How will you ever forgive me for being so stupid?"

"It's okay. Really."

He sighed.

"I'll call Greenough when we get into Chicago," she continued. Glasses, paperback book, Extra-Strength Tylenol for tension headaches—which, on second thought, she didn't need anymore. Instead of putting the bottle in her duffel, she threw it in the wastebasket. "And I'll beg for my job back."

"Really? And your apartment?"

"I'm sure my roommate will take me back. With open arms. Because I'm the only one who cooks, cleans, and takes out the garbage."

"Parking space?"

"I might not get it back because there's a long waiting list."

"I'll get you a parking place at my building."

"Thanks. I can't tell you how grateful I am. You really showed me just how stupid I am."

"That's what friends are for."

"Actually, TJ, I was just playing with you," Paige said, zipping her bag. "I'm not calling Greenough; I'm not going back to New York; and frankly, my apartment was never big enough to hold anybody's collection of Beanie Babies and most folks would agree my apartment's pretty large. For Manhattan."

His face fell.

She stood up, picked up her duffel, and slammed the door behind her.

Berte offered her a cup of coffee. And eggs, bacon, sausage, two kinds of toast, pancakes, and stewed fruit. Paige just took the coffee. She glanced out the window, beyond a bed of orange marigolds and brilliant red impatiens. In the drive, Herman's head was stuck under the hood of a Ford Mustang, its pale yellow body waxed to a high sheen.

Paige sipped her coffee, grateful that Berte seemed to expect no more than an occasional nod as she chattered about her neighbors, the weather, the vegetables growing in the backyard. Grateful because Paige had some thinking to do.

TJ had looked at her. For just a moment. In that way. That mysterious way. The way he looked at other women. The ones who were blonde, tall, curvy, and gainfully employed in the modeling industry. In the moment before he'd remembered that his dream included her in a white straitjacket.

Just before he'd said *straitjacket*.

No wonder women went nuts over him.

Because even though she was mad as hell at the

unceasing jabs about what she was choosing for her life, she couldn't deny that when he looked at her just that way . . . she was lost.

She glanced at her watch. Eight o'clock. At eight in Manhattan, she'd have put in an hour at the office. Her second cup of coffee would be stale. The dull throb at the back of her head would be spreading. And she would know, with great certainty, that she would lose a quarter of her to-do list to her clients' breaking emergencies.

There was no way she was going back—even if TJ would look at her just that way again. Or even twice more.

Three times? She wasn't sure she could hold out.

"OK, let's go," TJ's voice startled her. "Chicago by six tonight."

She glanced at her watch. In three minutes flat, he had shaved, brushed his teeth, and changed into an impeccably pressed oxford button-down shirt. He chugged his coffee, smiling at Berte in a way that made the woman's cheeks glow.

And made Paige even more aware of how she had been lucky, all these years, that he had never turned that charm on for her—a friend, a buddy, a pal. He wouldn't do it to her again. Wouldn't look at her like that again. If he did, she would melt. Just as every other woman did when he was around.

No. If he does it again, Paige thought, *I'm dropping him off at the nearest train station, bus terminal, or airport. Because if I don't, I'll be back at Greenough, Challenger & Redmond.*

To fasten her resolve, she burned the back of her mouth with the rest of her coffee.

"Ready to go?" she asked, all business.

He shrugged her duffel bag over his shoulder, thanked Berte for her hospitality, and left, the slam of the screen door echoing in his wake.

"That is some man," Berte said, shaking her head. "And you're not married to each other?"

"No."

"Not even a little bit of romance between you?"

"No, he's not my type."

"How could any woman on earth have a type that didn't include him?"

"I've seen too many women fall under his spell," Paige said dryly. "Medical science hasn't come up with a cure."

"Who needs a cure?" Berte sighed.

Paige thanked her hostess for her hospitality, a thank-you that was immediately countered with Berte's own gratitude that she would, courtesy of Paige's distress, soon be driving a new sports car.

The two women walked out to the driveway just as Herman slammed the hood shut.

"This baby won't give you a moment's trouble," he said. His smile was plain and friendly.

TJ held out his hand for the keys.

"Unh-unh," Herman said. "She's the one who gets the car."

Paige took the keys, accepted his courtly bow with her own graceful nod, and slipped into the driver's seat of the largest automobile she had ever had cause to be in. The car purred when she turned the ignition switch. TJ threw his bag in the backseat and climbed in beside her.

They pulled out of the driveway. Herman and Berte

stood side by side—Berte waving a dishtowel, Herman holding his hand up to the brim of his baseball cap.

"Thank goodness we're out of there," TJ said. "Horrible food."

"I thought it was fine."

"Paige, don't be sarcastic. I know you. You count every gram of fat, every molecule of salt. You must have been out of your mind with Berte's cooking."

"Not at all. Maybe it isn't so bad to eat without a calculator."

"But they don't eat salad. They've probably never had lettuce."

Paige shrugged.

"Well, you have to admit they're a strange couple."

"Maybe. But they're happy."

"So out of touch. They don't have cable. Don't have a computer. And Herman told me they don't even get a paper delivered."

"Sometimes when I read the paper I get worried and upset about things that are too far away for me to do anything about. Maybe that's not healthy."

"Paige, please, buy me a paper when we see a place to stop."

"You'll get carsick."

"That's an old wives' tale. I'll sit in the backseat—there's enough room back there to hold a meeting of the International Monetary Fund—and I'll read. It'll be just the way I read the paper every morning. Except my desk doesn't move."

He should have been suspicious when she pulled off at the highway rest stop and purchased six newspapers, three business monthlies, and a steaming hot capuccino in a styrofoam cup.

"Ah, heaven," he said, opening the front section of the *New York Times*.

Forty-five minutes later, he noticed his stomach felt kind of queasy. He ignored it. Ten minutes after that, he realized he had a throbbing headache settling behind his eyes. Another five minutes and the landscape seemed to be twirling around his head.

"Uh, Paige."

She stopped the car just in time.

When he got back from the field beyond the shoulder of the highway, she handed him a package of breath mints. He gargled with his capuccino and spit onto the shoulder of the road.

"Told you," she said. "It's not an old wives' tale. You really do get sick if you read in a car."

He looked up and noticed a green sign informing all travelers that the Jefferson County Fairgrounds were just ahead.

"Paige," he said slowly. "Where are we?"

"Just inside Ohio."

"I figured that. But we're not on Interstate 70."

"I thought we'd take the scenic route."

"I thought we'd get to Chicago."

"We will. Maybe we should stop for a while, you being sick and all."

He had to admit, the idea of the car moving, at all, made him want to heave again.

"I could go to the fair," Paige said. "You could sit in the car and recover."

"You have never had the remotest interest in fairs."

"I have always loved a good fair. And TJ, I just

want to spend an hour here. And then I'll drive straight through."

"No, I'll drive."

"All right, I'll make you a deal. You let me spend an hour at the fair and you can drive."

"Are you sure this isn't a plot to keep me from—"

"We've got so much extra time there's no way we're not going to make Chicago by six o'clock. That's when you're supposed to have dinner with Mr. Smith."

She started up the car, pulling onto the two-lane frontage road. It wasn't such a good idea.

"All right, fine," TJ said. "But I'm staying in the car."

"Suit yourself."

"One hour."

"Look, they have a Ferris wheel. And a merry-go-round."

"Merry-go-rounds are for kids, Paige."

"I'm feeling like a kid."

She parked the car.

"One hour, huh?"

"I don't trust you."

"What, me? I'll be back in an hour."

"I'll go with you," he grumbled. "Keep an eye on . . . hey, wait for me!"

He scrambled out of the car, checked to see if they could get back out of the grassy-field-turned-parking-lot, and caught up with Paige's adopted New Yorker stride.

"Isn't this great?" she asked excitedly. "Remember when we were kids and our parents would drive us down to Breckenridge for the fair? This is just like it."

It wasn't just like it, TJ thought. The Vail and Breckenridge and Aspen of his childhood were tall mountains, the crisp scent of earth and pine, the Ferris wheel tall and stately, the 4-H Club animals true wonders of nature. He had loved the summer fairs of the towns surrounding Sugar Mountain, but he hadn't thought of them for some time.

Every memory included Jack, and that meant it was put away. Never to be taken out. Except in the most melancholy of moments. The kind he snapped out of quickest.

He should go back to the car.

He hadn't even cracked open *Investor's Business Daily.*

He nearly pulled away from her when she took his hand. The crowd was dense, moving one way and then shifting another. Then the idea of losing her worried him—whether because he wouldn't make Chicago or because he simply wanted her near him, he couldn't have said.

He realized he had lost her. He shouldered past two matrons with a quick *excuse me* and put his arm around Paige's tiny waist.

"All right," he conceded. "One Ferris-wheel ride. One merry-go-round. That's it. Then we leave. Back on 70. None of this scenic-route stuff."

"Spinning Cup Ride?"

"Arrgh. Okay."

"Cotton candy?"

He wasn't sure he could think about food quite

yet, but his headache was clearing and the queasiness in his stomach was sure to follow.

"You drive a hard bargain. Cotton candy. But you have to eat it on the way back to the car. We're out of here in an hour, Paige."

"Absolutely!"

Her apple-green eyes twinkled with happiness. She smiled and he thought that some men could die happy if that smile was the last thing they saw.

Of course, Paige was just a friend, nothing more— so he wasn't affected by it in the same way that any other man would be. He just wondered idly how far she'd go to persuade him to stay longer.

Didn't matter. He'd hold firm.

One Ferris-wheel ride, one merry-go-round. All right, the Spinning Cups and then a cotton candy to eat on the way back to the car.

No smile from Paige, however charming, was going to change his determination to get to Chicago on time.

TEN

The carnie talked with a cigarette dangling perilously from his lower lip. He put the cigarette down only long enough to blow up a balloon and tie it with his teeth and the hand that wasn't holding the darts. Then he shoved his cigarette back in his mouth and tacked the balloon up on the bulletin board behind him.

Then he picked up another balloon and repeated the ritual.

Amazingly, he didn't set fire to his mouth, the balloons, or his tent.

"One balloon out, two tries, you get yourself one of 'em small beanies. Two balloons, two tries, pop up to medium beanie and I'll give you 'nuther dart. Pop a third, 'n you trade up to the next level; you get a larger one, give you 'nuther dart. Hightail to fourth and then you can have one of 'em giants," he said, tossing his head at the top shelf behind him where the stuffed animals were as big as the kids gathered around TJ and Paige. The carnie tacked another balloon up on the mosaic of red, yellow, and blue balloons. "Questions?"

Paige actually had a few, starting with could he repeat everything he had just said, but more slowly and possibly even without the cigarette in his mouth? But the pugnacious tilt of his chin made clear that the word *questions* was the functional equivalent of clearing his throat.

TJ handed her the rubber duck he'd won at the Pop 'Em and Stop 'Em booth, the alien he'd won at Rack 'Em and Stack 'Em, a mylar balloon, and the extra large cone of cotton candy Paige had eaten most of.

"I can get you the penguin," he said, pointing to the rafters of the carnie's booth. "I know you like penguins."

"I do?"

"Now that one'll cost you double darts," the carnie drawled. The ensuing explanation was long on charisma but short on sense. Still, Paige and TJ understood him to mean that all they had to do was hand over eight dollars, for which they would receive eight darts with which TJ was to puncture eight balloons. And the penguin would be theirs.

Paige shifted her prizes from one arm to another. The morning had turned into afternoon and the afternoon had turned hot. One Ferris-wheel ride had turned into two. And the merry-go-round and the Spinning Cups on the other end of the fairgrounds looked simply irresistible.

Not that Paige was complaining. She didn't have anyplace to be until the end of the week. And TJ was acting as if she were his best . . . pal, buddy, friend. The only time he'd touched her was to hold her hand on the roller coaster—and the rickety contraption was so stomach-squalling that anybody with a lick of sense would grab the hand of their seatmate and hold tight. The only time he looked directly at her, as near as she could tell, was in the fun house at the mirrors that made both of them look like roly-poly bowling pins.

They were back to their easy friendship; and Paige wondered if they had ever left that intimate, yet sexless, land.

Maybe he had just had some sleep in his eyes when he'd looked at her all funny this morning. Or a dust mote. Or maybe he needed glasses. Maybe she had imagined that whisper of desire—because she was feeling nostalgia or separation anxiety or even some regret about the choices she had made. Maybe it was how the sunlight had tumbled through the sieve of lace curtain. Maybe it was something unique to the Pennsylvania air playing tricks on her.

He didn't desire her, didn't think of her in any particularly sexual way, except to note that she used the ladies' room and he used the gentlemen's, that she wore a suit with a skirt and he didn't, and that she used lipstick and he didn't.

Pop! went the yellow balloon. And then another. The herd of boys watching TJ had swelled by ten and then twenty. Families stopped to crane their necks. Paige was pushed toward TJ, but then shoved back with the carnie's admonition to step back and let the man have some room, delivered with such vehemence that he nearly swallowed his cigarette.

Pop! TJ turned, winked at Paige, and gave her a this-is-how-it's-done smile that made a woman at Paige's shoulder sigh. A smattering of applause filtered up from the ground with the heat and dust.

"Folks, we may have a *bona fide* expert," the

carnie announced. "Just four more balloons and this man'll put me outa business. I'll have to pack up my tent and move on back to Florida."

Not any time soon if any onlookers were going to take their turns after TJ. A baby carriage shoved up into Paige's knee, and when she turned around she was given a quick apology by a mom who pulled back to give Paige room only to have three men slip into the opening.

"Could you do that?" one of them asked his pals.

"Nah, but you know that all these carnie things is rigged."

"They ain't rigged."

"It's just like professional wrestling."

"Wrestling ain't rigged!" Delivered with a healthy dose of indignation.

Paige moved away, shouldering through the family in front of her. She felt a mild tug as the alien doll TJ had won for her got caught up in a balloon string. But with a quick yank she was free.

Pop!

"This man's a genius with the dart!" the carnie crowed. "And he's just gotten his lady friend a fine plush penguin."

A healthy ovation was TJ's reward as the carnie used a hook to pull the penguin down from the rafters. As he handed it over to TJ, the carnie lit another cigarette and asked the crowd which one of them was ready with their money. The grinning believer in the intertwined sanctity of pro wrestling and carnival integrity stepped up to take his turn.

TJ squeezed through the crowd, accepting a couple of hearty slaps on the back and handshakes. He presented the penguin to Paige. His smile was both sheepish and proud.

"Now can we please get out of here?" he asked.

She didn't point out that it was he who had wanted to stay.

As they strolled out of the park, Paige handed the alien to a child who admired it. Gave the teddy bear to a boy who was visibly upset that he had failed at the ring toss. The mylar balloon she gave to an elderly woman sitting alone on a bench.

It was a custom that Paige and TJ had followed when they had gone to the summer fairs in the Colorado hinterlands—it was a given that winners shared their spoils with those who looked as if they might never get a turn to play.

But she kept the penguin, for that was special. When TJ took it from her for a moment to admire its silly grin, she felt as light as a feather, her hands free for the first time since they had parked the car.

Her hands free . . .

"TJ," she said, her heart thaddumping. "TJ, I gotta problem."

"What?" he asked, clearly torn between wanting to waste his last few tickets on the Cleopatra's Needle Ride and getting to the car.

"Someone took my purse."

He looked her up and down. The little leather shoulder bag didn't materialize. They looked back at the carnie's booth. The crowd had dissolved. The boy who had taken a turn after TJ wasn't doing such a good job. He had only his friends to admire and tease him.

"Oh, no," Paige groaned. "It's got everything. My credit cards, my driver's license, my money."

They scanned the horizon, both knowing that a purse snatcher was way ahead of them. Both were New York in their outlook, having had so many friends and neighbors who were the victims of crime.

"I wasn't thinking. Gosh, in the city, I would have held my shoulder bag in front of me. Would have watched it."

"Don't blame yourself," TJ said. "And it's really not that much of a problem. You can cancel credit cards. And money, well, I've got enough. And as for driving, I'm the one who's supposed to . . ." He reached into his back pocket. His very, very empty back pocket. "Uh, Paige, we've got a real problem."

Combined assets upon leaving the Columbia, Ohio, Police Station at seven-thirty:

1. A temporary driver's license issued to one Paige Burleson, a former resident of New York City.

2. A box of leftovers from a chicken dinner for three dropped off by Officer Bob Kerner's wife.

3. Twenty dollars borrowed from Officer Bob as well as his address in case the loan could be repaid, a notion that he dismissed and which TJ vigorously defended.

4. A stuffed penguin with what Paige now thought was an entirely too-smug grin.

5. A rain check for dinner from the president of SunOil.

"We'll catch you tomorrow night," Mr. Smith said when TJ called him from the station house. "You are coming tomorrow morning, aren't you? After all, the Motorcon people will be here to work out the final details. We'll be announcing that you'll be signing on as CEO in a consulting capacity. We can't do that if you're not here, and since that's an important element of the deal . . ."

TJ had nodded, propping the phone between his ear and a weary shoulder.

"Besides, Shawna's got her heart set on seeing you," the company president continued. And here TJ looked across the lobby to Paige, deep in conversation with Officer Bob's wife. "You two haven't seen each other in, what is it? A month?"

"Something like that."

"I don't approve of commuter marriages."

"Well, we're not exactly—"

"And both of you could do with some settling down. No extracurricular behavior, if you catch my drift."

"Mr. Smith!"

"My New York jeweler called me. Told me you'd been in and picked out a mighty fine diamond. I think you two will make a great team."

TJ gulped water from a glass on Officer Bob's desk.

"Mr. Smith, I think we should talk about—"

"Not now, not now. We'll talk tomorrow," the president concluded cheerily.

"I don't think Shawna and I are in love in that special way that—"

A dial tone was TJ's solace and reproach.

Shawna. The Oil-Me-Up Girl. Blonde, but not bottle blonde. Tall, but not so tall that she made a man feel like less of a man. Curvy, but just shy of vulgar—she could still be the girl-next-door, just a very well-developed girl-next-door. Brainy, but no one besides him had ever noticed. Ambitious . . . well, he'd never thought she was, but at least she never interfered with his ambitions.

She was everything, absolutely everything he had ever wanted in a woman. At least in the abstract. And she didn't seem to mind that he didn't love her, probably couldn't love any woman—at least not in the way that recipes like sonnets, songs, and syrupy sweet movies concocted.

He should marry her.

He shouldn't marry her.

He should marry her.

He was going to drive himself right up the wall if he kept thinking about it, going back and forth until his right brain and left brain felt like two sides of a Ping-Pong table.

He rubbed away a headache that was starting on the bridge of his nose and concentrated on the map on Officer Bob's desk. Seven hours, Bob had told him. Seven hours and he'd be in Chicago's Loop, parked in front of the Palmer House Hotel where his reservation lay unclaimed. Officer Bob had used a highlighter pen to mark out a straight-up, no-fail route to Chicago.

Take 70 until Indianapolis. Change over to Interstate 65. 70 would take them directly to Chicago.

"Now, the pretty lady has to drive," Officer Bob warned him. "Your license to drive in the state of New York expired seven years ago."

THE PUBLISHERS OF ZEBRA BOUQUET

are making this special offer to lovers of contemporary romances to introduce this exciting new line of novels. Zebra's Bouquet Romances have been praised by critics and authors alike as being of the highest quality and best written romantic fiction available today.

EACH FULL-LENGTH NOVEL

has been written by authors you know and love as well as by up and coming writers that you'll only find with Zebra Bouquet. We'll bring y the newest novels by world famous authors like Vanessa Grant, Judy Gil Ann Josephson and award winning Suzanne Barrett and Leigh Greenwood—to name just a few. Zebra Bouquet's editors have selected only the very best and highest quality romances for up-and-coming publications under the Bouquet banner.

YOU'LL BE TREATED

to tales of star-crossed lovers in glamourous settings that are sure to captivate you. These stories will keep you enthralled to the very happy end.

4 FREE NOVELS As a way to introduce you to these

terrific romances, the publishers of Bouquet are offering Zebra Romance readers Four Free Bouquet novels. They are yours for the asking with no obligation to buy a single book. Read them at your leisure. We are sure that after you've read these introductory books you'll want more! (If you do not wish to receive any further Bouquet novels, simply write "cancel" on the invoice and return to us within 10 days.)

SAVE 20% WITH HOME DELIVERY

Each month you'll receive four just-published Bouquet romances. We'll ship them to you as soon as they are printed (you may even get them before the bookstores). You'll have 10 days to preview these exciting novels for Free. If you decide to keep them, you'll be billed the special preferred home subscription price of just $3.20 per book; a total of just $12.80 — that's a savings of 20% off the publisher's price. If for any reason you are not satisfied simply return the novels for full credit, no questions asked. You'll never have to purchase a minimum number of books and you may cancel your subscription at any time.

GET STARTED TODAY –
NO RISK AND NO OBLIGATION

To get your introductory gift of 4 Free Bouquet Romances fill out and mail the enclosed Free Book Certificate today. We'll ship your free books as soon as we receive this information. Remember that you are under no obligation. This is a risk-free offer from the publishers of Zebra Bouquet Romances.

Call us TOLL FREE at 1-888-345-BOOK
Visit our website at www.kensingtonbooks.com

FREE BOOK CERTIFICATE

YES! I would like to take you up on your offer. Please send me 4 Free Bouquet Romance Novels as my introductory gift. I understand that unless I tell you otherwise, I will then receive the 4 newest Bouquet novels to preview each month FREE for 10 days. If I decide to keep them I'll pay the preferred home subscriber's price of just $3.20 each (a total of only $12.80) plus $1.50 for shipping and handling. That's a 20% savings off the publisher's price. I understand that I may return any shipment for full credit—no questions asked—and I may cancel this subscription at any time with no obligation. Regardless of what I decide to do, the 4 Free Introductory Novels are mine to keep as Bouquet's gift.

BN040A

Name _____

Address _____

City _____ State _____ Zip _____

Telephone ( ) _____

Signature _____

(If under 18, parent or guardian must sign.)

For your convenience you may charge your shipments automatically to a Visa or MasterCard so you'll never have to worry about late payments and missing shipments. If you return any shipment, we'll credit your account.

☐ Yes, charge my credit card for my "Bouquet Romance" shipments until I tell you otherwise.
☐ Visa ☐ MasterCard

Account Number _____

Expiration Date _____

Signature _____

Orders subject to acceptance by Zebra Home Subscription Service. Terms and Prices subject to change.
Order valid only in the U.S.

If this response card is missing,
call us at 1-888-345-BOOK.

Be sure to visit our website at
www.kensingtonbooks.com

BOUQUET ROMANCES
Zebra Home Subscription Service, Inc.
P.O. Box 5214
Clifton NJ 07015-5214

"I hadn't noticed. Didn't really need a car in the city."

"Yeah, but any police officer in the country will nail you on it. Let her drive. You navigate. If you have to be in Chicago on business, you take control of the situation. Keep this map on your lap at all times. Stay focused. Don't fall asleep. Don't let her get sidetracked. That's what's gotten you into trouble so far from what little I've gathered of the situation."

"Yes, sir. I mean, no, officer. I mean, yes, officer, you're exactly right."

"Call me *Bob*. Come on, I'll drive you back to the fairgrounds."

Paige and TJ rode in the backseat of the squad car. TJ felt her guilt, her self-reproach. It wasn't her fault, not really, at least everything after the kidnapping. He reached across the seat cushion and took her slender hand. His fingers curled over hers.

I'm sorry, she squeezed.

Nada, he squeezed back.

The fairgrounds rose in glowing neon splendor above the field. Jangling music and shrill screeches pulsed in time with the Viking Roll. They inhaled salty popcorn and sweat as it wafted into the squad car's open windows.

"Dang," Officer Bob said, sidling his car up to the shoulder of the road. "You're not getting your Mustang out until closing time."

TJ and Paige got out and surveyed the cars parked in a pattern as intricate as the most Byzantine maze. Herman's yellow mustang was trapped in its core.

"I could get on the loudspeaker and see if I can't get some of these people to get their cars outta the way," Officer Bob said doubtfully. "There's a minimum thousand dollars in tickets on illegal parking just sitting here waitin' for me to do something."

"Don't bother," TJ said.

"You need more money?" Bob asked. "I could give you a little more so you could go back in there and do a few rides you missed the first time."

"No way," TJ said. "I've had enough of fairs. Paige, are you interested?"

She shook her head.

"Well, I'd figure on an hour," Bob said. "Two hours tops. After the fireworks display, people'll clear out."

After he was gone, Paige and TJ walked to the car.

"Fireworks," TJ mused. "Let's put the top down."

Paige sat in the backseat, unfolding the blanket Berte had packed and tucking it over her legs. TJ jiggled with the radio stations until Paige teased him that he was just looking for financial reports.

"No, I'm not," he lied and put on a dusty Stevie Nicks to prove his words. "Although it is the first day in my adult life that I haven't known what's going on on Wall Street or the overseas markets."

"I'll toast to that," Paige said, hoisting a diet cola can up in the air.

He climbed over the seat, landing with his head on her lap. The sun disappeared behind the sprawling apple orchard across the street. Tiny white stars dotted a pale pink-and-blue evening sky. They looked beautiful, like diamonds. So did Paige. Before he could tell her, the fireworks began.

They could have been any couple in love. Watching

fireworks in the backseat of a convertible. His head on her lap. Her scent on his mind. They each pointed to explosions, declared them their favorites, and changed their minds when the next one was set off.

When the fireworks were over, citizens came for their cars. There was grumbling from folks who had to wait. Groans from those whose cars were trapped between others.

But all those bad feelings were canceled out with just as many *good nights* and *no, you firsts*. A goodly number of people in cars near the Mustang inquired if TJ and Paige wanted to start their car and go on ahead.

"No, thanks," TJ would reply. "We're just looking at the stars."

Officer Bob stood guard at the road shoulder with two flashlights to guide traffic. In twenty minutes it was over. Muddy tire tracks, a smattering of empty soda cans, a child's sweatshirt, a memory of headlights were all that was left on the field outside the carnival. Gentle moody music on the car radio, some station from Chillicothe, and the sounds of a carnival takedown.

"I think the Big Dipper is my favorite," TJ said. "It's a very no-nonsense constellation. Straightforward. Streamlined. Minimalist. Urbane."

"I've always been partial to the Little Dipper," Paige said.

"Dainty little thing, aren't you?"

She laughed.

He propped himself up on his elbow.

"You know, Paige, you're my best friend. I can't

imagine being stuck in the middle of nowhere with anyone else but you."

"High praise."

"No, really, I don't know what's been happening to us since we started this trip. We should do this more often. You know, road trips."

"With your schedule? And with what girlfriend tagging along?"

"Oh, Paige, I think maybe I need some time to reconsider my whole life. Everything I think. Everything I feel. Everything that is one way might really be another."

Words didn't do it.

Instinct took over.

He pulled her down to him.

Kissed her on the mouth, tasting popcorn salt and sweetness as his tongue entered the soft flesh of her lips. She moaned, at first in protest and then in pleasure. He would have let go if pleasure hadn't been on her lips, but now he couldn't, just couldn't, let her go.

It was so right, so absolutely right, so right that when he touched the gentle curve of flesh beneath her blouse, he knew she wanted him, too. . . .

ELEVEN

The car doors slammed in unison. TJ stood on one side of the big yellow Mustang. Paige on the other.

"Whoa," TJ exclaimed, rubbing his jaw.

"Mistake," Paige said firmly, planting her palms on the edge of the door.

"You think so?"

She nodded vigorously.

"Absolutely a mistake."

"I don't know. Actually, it felt pretty—"

"No, don't say it."

"Don't say it at all?"

"No, because it's too late for this."

"For what?"

"For a relationship."

"We already have a relationship. We've had one for years. That there thing in the car was a *kiss*."

They both looked at the backseat as if it were Cupid with an inch-thick rap sheet and hundreds of outstanding arrest warrants.

"It wasn't just a kiss."

"All right, so I touched your . . . your breast."

"We have a friendship," Paige said. "And that kiss wasn't friendly."

"That kiss was as friendly as all get-out."

"No it wasn't. It was more like . . . lust."

He put his right hand over his heart and held up his other hand as if he were swearing an oath.

"All right, counselor, I confess it was a lusty-as-all-get-out kiss. And a lusty-as-all-get-out feel. But I don't see what's wrong with it, with kissing and touching and taking things a little further."

Her eyes narrowed dangerously.

"How much further?"

"What kind of question is that? You're an adult; you know where this can go." He gestured broadly in the face of her squint. "Further."

"How much further? Are we talking making-love-much-further? Or just making-out-much-further?"

He tugged at his collar, which suddenly felt very, very tight.

"Making love would be nice," he said with a false nonchalance. "If that's what we both want. And I'll tell you something—I vote *yes*. Definitely vote *yes* to making love."

He squared his shoulders, regaining his balance. The kiss had been like stars popping off in his head—the Big Dipper, Little Dipper, all the medium-sized dippers in between.

He hadn't thought he could stand so tall, so proud; had instead put his weight on his hands, balancing on the side of the car.

But now that he had a purpose, now that he knew what he wanted and knew it was right, he stood high. Cocked his head back a little. Rested his elbow on the top of the windshield.

"I want you, Paige. And I think—no, I know—you

want me, too. Your lips don't lie. Your lips said *yes*. And so did your . . ."

She moaned. Then swayed against the car, looking pitifully afraid.

"Then we wouldn't be friends anymore."

"Maybe we can't be friends, darling. That wouldn't be the worst thing in the world."

She brought her lips together in a single disapproving line.

"Paige, maybe men and women can't really be friends," he said, warming to the notion. "Maybe there's always, you know, the possibility of lust between them. One of them wanting more than the other, just the way Herman explained. One of them complex and the other a randy animal with one thing on its mind. And you can guess which one I am."

The car stretched between them, a cavernous den of iniquity, a symbol of the base wants and desires that could destroy or delight them.

"And then one touch is all it takes," TJ continued. "And BAM! That's the end of friendship and the beginning of . . . something else."

She shook her head.

"I want you, Paige," he said softly. "And I think you want me, too."

"TJ, this is a bad idea," she replied cautiously. "It's too late for anything more than friendship. And what you're telling me is there's no real friendship. Not anymore. So everything I've believed in is false."

A single tear fell down her cheek.

"No, darling, I don't mean that. I just mean we both feel something more than buddy-buddy. And that it might be natural for men and women to want to take it further. It wasn't until this century that men and women even thought that they could be friends. We're actually being quite modern."

"No further," she said, shaking her head.

"Are you worried I won't call you the next morning? I can't not call you the next morning. I'm stuck in the middle of nowhere with you, and tomorrow morning I'll still be stuck in the middle of nowhere with you."

"It's not nowhere. It's Ohio," she corrected. "But what about the tomorrows after I get you to Chicago?"

He hated the distance between them, the metal and leather interior and inches that stretched into feet. If he had her in his arms, he could overcome her objections.

Another kiss was all it would take. Those nipples, hard beneath her t-shirt though it was a warm June night. Those cheeks, flush with wanting. Even the nervous drumming of her fingers on the car hood. A kiss was all it would take to heal the lips she bit so hard. One touch—and she'd be his.

But when he casually circled the car, she was a step ahead of him. He sidled up to the hood ornament. She sauntered to the back of the car and put two hands on either side of the trunk lock. He feinted right; she darted left. He made for left; she shook her finger at him like a teacher warning a kindergartner to settle down. They could have been two children playing musical chairs with a sports car.

"Look, Chicago is just a merger meeting," he said, putting two elbows on the trunk as if he intended to stay put. "You go on and have a great time at the reunion and then we'll both go back to New York. Together. It can be just as it was or it can be more. A lot more. It's up to you."

He thought of the diamond ring in a box that was in his jeans pocket. He could take it out right now. Ask her to marry him right then and there. That'd do it.

She was, after all, a serious sort of woman. Not the kind for flings and one-night stands—every guy he had ever set her up with had said as much, and the ones who said they didn't like that got a BACK-OFF from TJ that was not to be questioned.

Marry her. Yeah, marry her.

He smacked his forehead. Marriage! What was he thinking of? A week ago this was his best friend and nary a domestic thought for her had entered his head. Marriage? With Paige it would be a real marriage, not the sort of arrangement Shawna had suggested.

Irrational to ask her. Out of his mind to be thinking that far ahead. Not like him to jump impulsively into something. Besides, it had to be a five-to-ten-in-the-pen etiquette violation to give her a diamond that the jeweler had sold him for another woman.

"You're forgetting something," Paige said, popping the bubble on his fantasy. "TJ, I'm not coming back to New York."

"Well, sure, when we're just friends, you can't be expected to stay in a city in which you're not happy just to be with me. But now things are different."

"But that's what I've been doing all along."

"I'm talking about after we're—"

"I'm not going back."

"Ever?"

"Ever."

"What about Connecticut? Westchester? Long Island? We could live in any of those places. I'll get a driver's license. I'll buy a car or take a train into Manhattan. I'll work at home two days a week. I can be as modern as all get-out as long as we're very traditional about one thing."

"What one thing?"

"When we go to sleep, we do it in the same bed."

She shook her head.

"I'm going back to Sugar Mountain. It might be for good. And another thing, I made love to you once and I wanted to believe I could put that night in a box and close the lid tight. I thought I did it," she said. Her voice cracked. "But it changed the course of my life, made me picky about men, made me take a job in New York, made me choose law when deep in my heart I think people ought to be able to solve their problems in a less adversarial fashion. I don't want you making love to me because I don't want my life going off in a direction I can't control. You're not responsible for what I do, but I am. And I am fully in control of myself. I am not having an affair with you. Not now. Not ever."

She boldly met his gaze. Her face was pale and composed. Her hands rested lightly and delicately on the hood of the car. Her apple-green eyes stared at him boldly—he knew he couldn't risk checking out her breasts for any sign of bodily rebellion. He met her gaze steadily. She was the first to break. She looked down. He followed her gaze.

He sighed. Tried to think about cold things—ice cream, igloos, snowmen, skating rinks—until the

June evening seemed more like January, his cheeks felt cool not flush, and his pulse didn't race quite so hard.

"We'd better drive," he concluded. "Because that backseat is wicked trouble."

"Give me the keys. You don't have a license. And besides, it's my car."

Switching sides, they passed each other. TJ caught her sleeve. His scent was of pine and citrus, but with an undercurrent of scent that was sharply evocative, taking her back five, no ten, years ago. She had made love to him once, asking nothing of the future. But the future had asked much of her, sending her on a long, long detour of her life. For that was all that New York was for her now—a detour.

"Too late?" he whispered huskily.

She nodded.

"Too late."

His hands, flexed and so close to taking her, fell to his sides. Limp and defeated. A puzzled look, barely visible in moonlight and the dormant Ferris-wheel lights. She sympathized. Things were never out of his reach; things were always possible to obtain. Hard work or charm. Long hours or a smile. Whatever TJ had wanted in life, he got. Sometimes it was easy, sometimes difficult, but always obtainable.

And she wondered suddenly if he hadn't always figured her for his. Better as a friend, of course. But always there. Always there to be the fifth man in a pickup game of basketball, always there for a quick dinner after a late night at the office, always there for holidays, always dependable for an emergency.

She wished she could still give that dependability

to him. Now . . . and forever. But she wanted things out of life. Things he couldn't give her.

She didn't look forward to facing Sugar Mountain on her own. But she'd do it. Do it and then figure out what to do with the rest of her life.

"Too late," she repeated and slipped out from between him and the hood of her new car.

She slid onto the driver's seat and turned the ignition key. He got in beside her.

"Map's in the glove compartment," she said, all business. "I don't usually stop off in Chicago; so, could you help me out a little?"

A half hour of silence later, Paige sighed.

"You know, Sugar Mountain is going to be so beautiful this time of year. The carpet of bluebells and black-eyed Susans. The air is so fresh and clean. Not like New York. And listening to Mayor Stern play the trumpet. Funny how a weekend away can refresh a person."

"Don't."

"Don't what?"

"Don't try to persuade me."

"Fine. Then don't persuade me to come back to New York."

"Agreed."

They shook hands.

"So, what do you want to talk about?" TJ asked.

In awkward silence, they jumped 70 for Interstate 65, heading northwest to Chicago. She glanced at TJ. He stared out the windshield, his jaw rippling, deep in thought. He noticed her scrutiny and turned on the radio station. He found a business station. A deep male voice announced closing numbers of the currencies around the world. The ruble, the yen, the peso, the dollar . . .

"I can't listen to any more of that," Paige said, flipping the station dial. "That's going to put me to sleep."

"It's important information."

"Fine. Then listen to it in Chicago," she said, and found a pleasant music station.

"If I hear that song one more time . . ." TJ warned. "It's been on the charts forever. And she's so lame as a singer."

"Okay, okay, you're right."

She flipped through the static until she hit a talk-radio show. The subject: Washington politics.

"Yuck," they both agreed.

She flipped off the radio.

The silence was sharp and accusatory.

"Hey, Paige, remember this?" TJ said, and started singing the Shaker hymn that had been their school song. " 'Tis a gift to be simple, 'tis a gift to be free, 'tis a gift to be just where you're supposed to be."

For a moment she didn't recognize the Sugar Mountain Elementary school song.

"I'm surprised you remember."

"We sang it every assembly and every year at the reunion weekend. It's tough to get out of my head. Funny thing, though, I tried to think of the song night before last when we were at that motel. I couldn't do it. Now, it's all I hear."

"A gift to be simple, 'tis a gift to be free."

"Paige, what are you going to tell your parents?"

She stopped singing.

It was going to be hard facing her father. Taking

the bank away from him—it was the thing he valued most, having opened its doors when he was fresh out of college. And facing the citizens of Sugar Mountain who had been affected by his decline wouldn't be easy. Sure, they'd understand but Sugar Mountain had never been given its fair share of the boom years and Paige hated to be the one to tell them to tighten their belts even further. She felt the familiar impulse of wanting to tell TJ everything—but she squelched it, biting her lip until she tasted salt.

She could tell him now. Tell him about his mother. It was the perfect opening. But she kept silent. Didn't want him to bolt from the car, which he would. She knew he would.

"What am I going to tell my parents?" she mused aloud. "Nothin'. I'll just show up. Tell them I want my old room back."

"Tired?" He asked hours later, handing her the soda can after a healthy swig. He could feel the caffeine touching the back of his head. He didn't need it to stay awake, but she did.

She took a gulp and nodded.

"It's okay. Two hours and I'll be dropping you off in front of your hotel."

Her voice sounded thick. Whether from tiredness or from lack of use of her vocal cords, he couldn't say. The silence of the past hours had been a harsh *gulag*. He didn't want the time to think—he wasn't a thinker as much as a man of action. Thinking about SunOil, its president, and the glamorous blonde Oil-Me-Up Girl.

He knew what he'd say about the market: It will be good to SunOil.

He knew what to say about Motorcon: Fantastic buy, like picking up gold at ten cents an ounce when it's trading at four-fifty dollars on the Swiss trading floors.

Consulting Chief Executive Officer of SunOil: An honor.

But Shawna? He knew what was expected; he knew the upside and the downside, just as surely as he did any number of business mergers and acquisitions. But now the most rational part of his life had become the most irrational. Lord, just kissing Paige once made him lose track of all the good reasons for marrying Shawna.

He looked at Paige's profile. Something she had said came back to him. *Picky about men.* Picky about men. She said she was picky about men. Lord knew it was true. Men were always too short, too tall, too conceited, too driven, not driven enough—and what else was it that Paige had said? She was picky about men because they had made love that once so long ago.

"I can do some driving," he said. "You got to get some sleep. You're looking weary."

"You don't have a license," Paige said. "You can't drive."

"I can drive," he insisted. "I just won't speed."

"You're the one who wants to get to Chicago awfully quick."

"Fifty-five will still get me in before the morning's meeting."

"You'll have to shave. Get your suit pressed. And you need a shower."

"Manageable. Come on, I've always done better than you on going without sleep."

"Okay," she said, turning over the keys. "But don't blame me if you get pulled over. You know, state troopers don't take kindly to folks driving without a license."

"I'm sure I can talk my way out of any ticket."

"I didn't want to speed, officer," TJ said. "It's just the truck behind me was so close. I was getting tailed."

"Just give me your license, sir. Sir?"

TJ's mouth tightened.

"I don't have one."

"You know, sir, we in Indiana don't take kindly to folks driving without a license," the young, well-shaved trooper said. "I'm afraid I'm going to have to ask you to step out of the vehicle."

TJ unbuckled his seat belt and opened the door. The trooper stepped aside to give him room to get out. He waved his flashlight over the car.

Paige slept in the backseat, one arm thrown over a stuffed penguin.

"Does she have a license?" he asked. "If she does, perhaps you should have had her drive."

"She was tired. I was worried about her."

"Well, sir, you really shouldn't drive without a license. You could have stopped at a hotel," he said, and noted TJ's expression. "Sir, it's not that outrageous a suggestion."

"Maybe not to most folks."

"May I see your vehicle registration and then we'll wake her up?"

"Sure."

TJ walked around to the passenger-side door and opened the glove compartment. That's where he'd put a vehicle registration if he had one for this car. But the glove compartment was clean, not even a gum wrapper or a map.

"That Herman," he said. "Maybe he gave it to Paige and she put it in her purse."

The officer waved a beam of light over the back of the car. No purse in sight.

"I forgot. She got her purse stolen."

"Sir, this might involve a trip to the station."

TJ looked up at the wide brim of the officer's hat.

"Is there any way we can avoid a ticket?"

"I think we're beyond that stage."

"A trip to the station?"

"I think so, sir."

"We can't work this out between us? I mean, I'm a businessman and one thing I've always tried to do is work things out on a more personal level."

The trooper's eyes narrowed.

"What are you suggesting?"

"Anything that would get me on the road. See, I'm from New York and I'm due in Chicago in a few hours and I can't really afford another trip to a police station."

"What do you mean—another?" The trooper asked, pulling handcuffs from his belt.

TWELVE

"Talk your way out of anything, huh?" Paige said as they left the station house.

"Hey, at least I'm not in jail."

"Only because it turns out you didn't have anything in your pocket to bribe a trooper with."

"I didn't want to bribe him," TJ said irritably, thinking that the only good part was that Paige hadn't been allowed back in the processing area when he was searched.

The state trooper had opened the velvet box, glanced back at the waiting room where Paige paced, and come to his own conclusions. TJ was released with just a warning—and a good-luck-man-hope-she-says-yes—and a tip of the trooper's brim.

"I just want breakfast now," he said, pausing to look in the window of an empty, darkened diner. "We can eat and wait for the pound to open so we can get your car back. Then we'll hit the road."

"I checked with the desk sergeant. We don't get Herman's car back."

"But they called Herman," TJ said. "They know it's not stolen."

"They won't release the car until Herman sends them the title."

"Have him fax it."

"He doesn't have a fax machine. He thinks his cousin in the next town over has one at his gas station. He'll call him at seven. It's now just four o'clock in the morning. If he faxes the title, the desk sergeant said we could have the car back by ten, with all the paperwork. That's still not going to get you to Chicago in time. Even if Herman's cousin has a fax machine."

"So I've blown the biggest meeting in my career because nobody has the technology to send a simple piece of paper across state lines." He groaned, rubbing his sandpaper-rough jaw. He caught his reflection in the drugstore window. Wished he had taken acting classes in college. Pulled his lips down in a stern frown. "You know, I need sleep." He crossed the street and headed right. Pointed to a little bed-and-breakfast that the trooper had told him about. "Lookee, there! Why don't we check in and get some shut-eye?"

"Absolutely not," she said sternly.

"Just sleep. Breakfast. Phone calls. A shower."

"We could get in trouble."

He almost told her he liked trouble. Especially the horizontal kind. But he didn't. No more teasing Paige. She was about as much fun as a schoolmarm.

"Paige, we can't do anything about getting to Chicago in time for the meeting. Let's get some sleep, a shower, some coffee, and I'll call Smith when it's decent and tell him I've blown it."

"Why aren't you more worried about missing your meeting?"

"Because it's important, but it's not important

enough to . . . if I don't get some sleep right away, I think I won't make it."

She looked as if she might try to take his temperature with a palm to his forehead. Maybe he could get an Oscar. He rubbed his stomach and groaned.

"We can make that meeting," she snapped. So much for acting. "We can walk to the highway. We can probably get you to Chicago in time. You need to make that meeting if you're going to be CEO of the SunOil conglomerate."

She passed the bed-and-breakfast. The front porch light was on. The proprietor, the trooper's mother, had told her son she'd leave the key under the mat. They could have the third-floor Bridal Suite.

Waste of a good room, that was.

TJ caught up to Paige.

"You think we're going to walk all the way to Chicago?"

"Hitchhike."

"That's too dangerous for a woman. Lot of crazy people out there."

"You'll be with me."

"If I'm standing with you they won't stop."

She regarded him speculatively. He had a point. He looked worse for wear. A single day's stubble had turned into a shaggy, prickly beard. His shirt, tailored by one of the finest custom shops in New York and once pressed to a starchy finish, was missing two buttons and had an unsightly oil stain, origin unknown. His hair needed a good comb—but Paige wasn't in the mood to run her fingers through it.

"Maybe you should step back from the road," she suggested.

"Paige, hitchhiking is not a good idea. We can just wait at the bed-and-breakfast . . . hey, wait for me!"

She marched quickly down the entrance ramp, not giving a thought to the first raindrop that hit her face. *Get TJ to Chicago. Get him to his meeting,* she ordered herself, wiping rain from her cheek.

Then she'd hightail it back here to get her car and she'd make the rest of the journey to Colorado. Or maybe she shouldn't, given what was waiting for her. Maybe she could go somewhere else, somewhere to start a new life.

But her family needed her. Needed her, even if her father didn't want her. How she dreaded telling her father that he had to turn over the keys to his office! It would break him.

Well, it was almost done. Almost over. Get TJ to Chicago; get him to his meeting; put him in the hands of SunOil's president and his daughter, the Oil-Me-Up Girl, and clear out.

The rain was coming down harder now and TJ stripped down to a t-shirt, throwing his button-down over Paige's shoulders. She glanced back at him in mute gratitude and saw behind his shoulder a set of headlights. She stuck out her thumb.

"Paige, step back, please," TJ warned. "This guy's not going to stop. Paige, please."

But she was determined that something, something about this trip, would work out right. She held her ground, even as the truck's headlights blinked a warning—accompanied by a roaring horn.

TJ jerked her back from the shoulder of the highway just as the eighteen-wheeler's tires punched them with a puddle of cold, muddy water. The force of the blow threw them backward, down an embankment to a swamp-grass ditch. TJ landed first and broke her fall. He clasped his arms around her.

"You know, Paige, this has not been an easy trip," he said.

She groaned. Wiped a slick mat of grass from her face. Pushed gritty mud out of her mouth with her tongue. Tried to get up. He held her tight; and if she had been paying more attention to him than to the fact that her shirt was ripped wide open, she would have known that he was doing some major thinking, plotting and planning.

"Let's just for one moment pretend we're comfortable," TJ said. "In a nice warm bed with thick, soft sheets and a telephone on the nightstand to call room service. We've just taken a hot shower and dried each other with big, fluffy towels."

He opened his eyes.

And met two unblinking green eyes.

"How 'bout if we pretend that this has been a pleasure trip?" he demanded. "And that you didn't trick me with some cockamamie story about a recluse with money. That you didn't kidnap me. That you weren't trying to drag me back to a high school reunion that I'd already said I didn't want anything to do with. And right now, I'm saying that the meeting in Chicago is not so important that I want to get thrown off the highway for it."

She jerked away from him. His shoes and socks were soaked. The rip on her shirt flapped open to cold, wet air. His shoulder hurt like hell from the fall. He knew he smelled like dirt and grass and exhaust.

"All right, I'm sorry!" Paige cried.

"Gotta be pretty damn sorry."

"I am."

"Sorry enough to go back to that bed-and-breakfast?"

"Get up," Paige snarled, standing and extending a hand. "I'm gonna try again. We're getting you to Chicago. This morning."

He let her think she was helping him get up. When he felt the pain in his ribs, he realized she really was helping. He couldn't make it on his own.

"You're the Wall Street Tiger, TJ! You're the one who's so damned determined to devote your life to business that you don't even have a life anymore."

"All I want is a comfortable bed, a hot shower, and clean clothes. That little bed-and-breakfast up there by the station house has a key under its mat. And I think after all I've been through because of you, you ought to at least have the decency to—"

He looked up at the shoulder of the road, illuminated in the headlights of an oncoming car. She had her thumb out.

"To what?" She yelled over the approaching rat-a-rat-a-rat-a of a muffler gone bad.

A late-model Cadillac passed, honking imperiously.

"Oh, damn, not again," TJ thought.

His eyes met those of the driver, a woman, who stared in horror as he emerged from the thick grass to grab hold of Paige. This time they didn't tumble.

"See, this isn't going to work," TJ said, pointing at the caddy. "Hitchhiking is a stupid idea. Let's go back to the bed-and-breakfast. Wouldn't you like . . . wouldn't you like . . . you like . . ."

"TJ, what's the matter with your voice?"

"Nothing," he said, clearing his throat. "It's just, Paige, I would never have guessed you were the type to wear a leopard-print bra."

She glanced down at the gash in her shirt. Faintly visible in the orange sodium glow of the highway lights was the trademark pattern of a wild and lascivious beast. The Cadillac was gone, long gone.

"All right, maybe hitchhiking isn't such a good idea," she growled, tugging her shirt together. "I need sewing supplies."

"I need something and it doesn't have anything to do with needles and thread," he said so softly she didn't hear him.

"Where'd you say this bed-and-breakfast is?" Paige tossed over her shoulder.

Through the thin white cotton of her t-shirt, he could just make out the contours of a black bra strap. He'd follow that little bra strap anywhere.

The key was under the mat, just as the trooper had said. The porch light was on, so TJ had no trouble opening the door. Quietly, quietly they tiptoed into the front foyer that smelled faintly of caramel and mothballs. On a maple wood sideboard was a wicker tray containing a plate of cookies, two glasses of milk, and a note saying, "My son said to tell you that they'll call you when the car is ready".

TJ took a cookie.

"Shhhh! Don't chew so loud."

She picked up the tray and stepped across the foyer. Groaning and creaking floorboards threw up their protest. She slipped off her dirty shoes and extended a toe to delicately step on the first stair. The screech was hideous.

"Don't bother trying not to make a lot of noise," a woman said. TJ looked up to see a woman, adorned with red jumbo-sized curlers, peering over the landing. "Floorboards in this house always creak. I figure that I can't ever be robbed because I'd know the culprit was in my house before he'd get to anything worthwhile."

TJ guiltlessly finished his bite of cookie. Chocolate chip with crunchy walnuts.

"I'm so sorry we're disturbing you," Paige apologized, coming up to the second floor. "And we're very grateful."

"No problem. My son sends over lost tourists and DUIs who need to sleep it off all the time."

The woman seemed to become aware of Paige's decolletage.

"That's a mighty pretty bra," she said. "Victoria's Secret?"

Paige turned around to find herself face-to . . . well, face-to-bra with TJ. He looked up at her with a cherubic grin—after all, if you put a gash in your t-shirt hitchhiking on a lonely highway, you deserve to have everyone comment on your choice of underwear.

"Yes," she confessed through tight lips. "Victoria's Secret."

My, my, never knew you even looked at that catalog, TJ thought. *And after all these years of my telling you you oughta try it.*

"I got my own VS credit card," the woman said. "How 'bout you?"

"Uh, I don't think I—"

"I'll show you and your husband your room. Do you have any luggage?"

"No, ma'am," TJ said.

"He's not my husband," Paige said.

The woman stopped. Turned around. Looked at both of them. Sternly. As sternly as a referee in a wrestling match that wasn't going by its preordained plan.

"I have one room left in this house and I quite firmly believe in marital values. If you all ain't married, one of you'd better leave now."

Won't be me, Paige said without words. She looked down two steps to TJ.

Won't be me, TJ stared up at her.

"Married," TJ said.

"Married," Paige confirmed, crossing her fingers behind her back.

"That's awfully nice. You look like such a sweet couple. Now, how 'bout if I loan you a little nightie and a t-shirt for when you head out of here?" their innkeeper asked. "I got them from the Victoria's Secret catalogue just last month."

"That'd be very nice," TJ said. "Wouldn't it, darling? My little wife loves Victoria's Secret. Buys from it all the time."

Having no other resources at her disposal to express her displeasure, Paige stuck her tongue out at him.

He blew her a kiss.

They were presented with the third-floor bedroom,

a charming little hideaway with a gabled roof, four-poster bed, and a nightstand. TJ took the tray of cookies from Paige, scrunched his head down into his shoulders so he wouldn't hit the ceiling, and closed the door behind him. While the innkeeper got Paige a nightie and a new t-shirt, he shucked off his dirty jeans, shirt, and socks. He jumped under the covers just as she came into the room.

She held up a piece of fabric that could have been a cocktail napkin.

"What's that?"

"My new nightie," Paige said. "I couldn't very well refuse her. Or ask for something a little more . . . more."

"Wow. I like it. Try it on."

She gave him a look. A not-in-your-dreams look.

"What about the t-shirt?" he asked.

"Close your eyes. No peeking."

When she was done putting it on, she gave a pitiful moan.

He opened his eyes. The t-shirt that the state trooper's mother had given her was constructed of a mesh fabric that would no doubt be quite helpful in catching tuna or other large fish on the high seas. However, it left something to be desired as a shirt. Over a leopard print bra. At least, some people would think it left something to be desired. TJ wasn't one of those people. He thought it showed off something to be desired very nicely.

"It's really quite . . . charming," he said, coughing dryly.

"I look like a tramp."

Since she looked as if she could pose for the catalog from which her attire came, he decided not to argue the point.

"Maybe if you wore my shirt over it."

"If I did, you wouldn't have a shirt. Which, by the way, you don't seem to have on."

"Fancy that," he said, looking down at his bare chest.

"You're sleeping on the floor. So get out from under the covers."

"I slept on the floor last night and the night before last. Tonight, I sleep in a bed. I deserve to sleep in a bed."

"Then I'll sleep on the floor."

"Paige, there isn't enough room on either side of this bed to put a human body. Please, just get into bed. I'm not an animal. I won't do anything. I'll stay on this side. You just make sure you stay on your side."

"Close your eyes again."

He did. Heard her unzip her jeans. The tug of the fabric. The swish-swish of her legs as she shimmied out of the jeans and then kicked them out from under her. His throat went dry.

"Can I open my eyes now?"

"Not yet."

She lifted the covers. He felt a brief caress of cool air and then warmth as she settled into the mattress. Their bodies did not touch. He dared not move.

"You know," he said, licking his chapped lips, "I never used to think of you as sexy. I never put you and sex together in the same thought."

"I'm the same way."

"It was almost as if we put that one night out of

our minds. I've thought of you as one of the guys. Just a pal. A buddy. A guy to play golf with. Somebody to shoot hoops with."

He opened one eye. She didn't scold him. He relaxed a little, letting his hand drop naturally to his side.

"Someone to go to the movies with," she said. "Someone to talk to. Someone to spend rainy afternoons with. You know, the kind of afternoons where you feel like reading a book by a fireplace."

"We haven't done that in a long time. Anyhow, I'm feeling all funny. Like right now. I know you're a female," he said. "A damn beautiful female. I knew it all along; I just hadn't figured it out. You know what I mean. And I don't know how it's going to affect our . . ."

He glanced over. Her eyes were closed, dark lashes leaving a shadow on her cheeks.

Her breathing was rhythmic and slow. Her eyes were closed. Her fingers were coiled around the lace edge of the sheet. He picked up her hands. Pulled the sheet out from her grasp. Lifted it for just one instant.

Whistled softly.

Put the sheet back in place. Smoothed it out.

"Wow, matching panties," he sighed.

And then he decided that he'd better sleep on the floor, even if there were only an inch on either side of the bed.

He wedged himself between the wall and the calico dust ruffle. Tried not to think about anything sexy, anything to do with Paige. Or leopard-print panties.

No, no, he thought, looking at his watch. Four-twenty-five in the morning.

Okay, he'd spend two-and-a-half hours staring up at the ceiling.

He'd list celebrities whose last names started with the same letter as their first names. Alan Alda, Barbi Benton, Cyd Charisse, church, church, church . . .

Again, he found himself in a church, at the altar, waiting for his bride.

THIRTEEN

That woman. In a white dress. Gliding down the aisle. Her black bra strap showed through the shimmering gossamer fabric.

He didn't wait for the minister.

Didn't wait for the vows.

He took her in his arms.

He woke up. The sunlight was streaming through lace curtains. His hand was around her waist. His legs spooned against hers. His face in her hair. She jerked upright. He sat up. How had he gotten into bed? However it was, he was getting right back out.

"Sorry," he mumbled.

Paige grabbed her jeans from the floor and managed to put them on, zipping them up without once giving him another gander at her panties.

"It's six-forty-five," she said. "Let's get over to the police station."

She slid out from under the covers and slammed the bathroom door behind her.

TJ stretched.

Obviously, they were not going to talk about this waking-up-in-the-same-bed business.

Which was fine with TJ. Because he had more experience than Paige did. He knew where this was going to end. It was just a matter of time. He'd be patient.

Because once they made love, she'd be his.

Forever.

"Sorry," the desk sergeant said. The brim of his cap barely hid his open admiration of Paige and her new mesh t-shirt. "Your Mr. Herman says there is no fax machine at his cousin's station. He thinks he can mail the title. But that's going to take a couple of days. He also said he could drive out here. He could probably make it in, say, three hours, earliest."

"Why can't you just accept his word and let us have the car?" Paige asked. A lock of her hair fell forward, across her ripe, green eyes. She could not have been more sexy if she had had staples across her stomach and a month to call her own.

The desk sergeant opened his mouth like a baby bird in a nest waiting for the worm from its mother's mouth.

TJ didn't like that look.

"Paige, rules are rules. They need the paperwork before they can give us the car. Why don't we go back to bed and . . ." TJ said. He did a double take. Paige was halfway down the hallway. "Paige, it's okay about the meeting. Really. I'll call Chicago. It's all right if I'm late."

He looked down at the desk sergeant.

"Don't look at my woman like that again."

"Sorry. I couldn't help it," the sergeant said, tugging at his collar. "It was that leopard print showing right through the t-shirt. It made me feel all funny inside. Like a, like a, I suddenly became like a—"

"Like an animal," TJ snarled. "I know. I feel the same way, too. But just 'cause I understand what you're going through doesn't mean I'm okay with you gawking at her."

"Okay, okay. But you'd best catch up with her, because she's going to cause a swivel-headed, rubbernecking, gawk-and-squawk traffic jam if she's out on the street by herself."

The highway. The damn highway. Route 65 off Interstate 70. Straight on to Chicago.

She walked right past the bed-and-breakfast inn, right past the park where two lovers could while away an hour just lying on the grass and soaking up the rays, right past the sign saying, "You Are Leaving Middlefork. Have a Safe and Pleasant Trip and Come Back Soon!"

TJ cursed the highway.

"Paige, we're not hitchhiking."

"Yes, we are."

She turned around on the shoulder, stuck out her thumb, and smiled.

That's when all hell broke loose.

The highway was not very busy—sure, there were trucks trying to make good time, farmers who didn't think seven was all that early, and assorted commuters who had to roar out of the garage at dawn to make their desks in Chicago by nine. Every vehicle had some place to go and every driver wanted to get there in a hurry.

But destinations took a backseat to the consternation caused by the sexy, sweet damsel in distress. And the road seemed mighty crowded with knights in shining armor.

"Need a ride, sister?"

"No, she doesn't," TJ said to the leering driver of a six-wheeler that had stopped on a dime. The trucker uttered a bad-tempered oath and roared away.

"Why'd you do that?"

"I didn't like the looks of him."

A late-model Pontiac rumbled to a stop on the shoulder.

"Where you off to, young lady?" asked its driver, slamming his door. He wore a plaid blazer, gray slacks, and a bad toupee. When he waddled up to Paige and TJ, he brought with him the distinct smell of garlic.

"Chicago," Paige said.

"I can get you as far as Chicago. I'm on my way to Minneapolis, but I don't mind a detour to help out a pretty lady."

"You'd have to take me," TJ countered. "And I have to sit in the front seat. And the last man who looked at my sister here like that got me five-to-ten years in the big house."

The driver got back in his car without another word.

Pickup trucks, station wagons, milk wagons, motorcycles, sedans. Many stopped; all were sent on their way.

"TJ, you are not helping matters by being so impolite," Paige said after a particularly blistering encounter between TJ and the driver of a bakery delivery truck who had offered to take the day off work to drive Paige (alone) to Chicago. "They'd take you along if you weren't so grouchy."

"I'm not grouchy. I'm just being protective."

"You're just being a jerk."

She stuck out her thumb.

"Lord Almighty, I never thought I'd see the day—but you've turned into a man magnet."

"Just because I'm wearing this stupid shirt?"

"No, it's everything," he said, looking her up and down. "It's your hair falling in your face; it's your breasts so darned . . . out there. And your jeans, they show off a lot of curves. But there's something else, too. When you were in New York, you gave off business vibes, a professional aura, something that said *treat me with respect.*"

"And now?"

"Now you're a walking, talking advertisement for the female sex."

"Really?"

"Doesn't that bother you?"

Paige gave it some thought. Certainly, she was used to being treated as a professional, with all the deference and respect that came with a degree and a nice office. She had worked hard to be treated seriously.

But now . . .

A green Army truck drove past; and while it didn't stop, it did make its approval of Paige known by horn, catcall, and one young soldier hanging out the back to blow her a kiss. Paige waved back at him.

"No," she concluded. "It doesn't really bother me."

"That does it," TJ said, tearing off his shirt. "Put this on."

"Now we'll never get a ride."

"That's fine with me. I'd rather stand out here on the highway for a week than take my chances with some of these animals."

She put on the shirt, which went down to her knees. It made a considerable difference in highway safety. But it didn't make TJ any less comfortable. And not just because he was shirtless.

"Paige, I'm not sure I'll ever be able to remember that you're not the opposite sex."

It was at this moment that a large green belching Ford Escort slowed to a stop on the shoulder just one hundred feet ahead of them.

Paige ran up the shoulder to meet the car. All TJ could do was follow.

The woman driver leaned over the bench seat and rolled down her window.

"Where are you-all headed?"

"Chicago," TJ said.

"The Palmer House Hotel," Paige added.

"Get in," the woman instructed them.

Paige and TJ climbed in. TJ slammed the car door shut a bare second after the woman's foot hit the accelerator.

"My name's Janice," she said and she nodded in the rearview mirror at their introductions. "I work at a bakery on the West Side of Chicago. Gets so hot and sweaty that me and the other girls on shift take turns bringing in towels to wipe the sweat off. Then we take them home to launder. Sorry about having to crowd you two together."

She glanced back.

"It's all right, thank you," TJ said.

"You only got one shirt between you?"

"Yeah, but she needs it more than I do."

"There's one of my son's undershirts in the laundry basket. You can try it on."

"Thanks."

TJ put on the undershirt. It was sleeveless and tight, but it did the job.

"Thanks, Janice."

"What business you got at the Palmer House? That's a fancy-pants kind of hotel."

"I have a meeting there," he said.

"I see," Janice said, seeming to think the better of the words *yeah, right.* "And what about you?"

"Oh, I'm not going to the meeting," Paige said. "I'm going to my high school reunion."

"Well, you might consider changing your clothes before you get there."

"Janice, ma'am, do you think you could drop us off at the hotel?" TJ asked, trying for a charming smile in the rearview mirror. He needed a shave. And a haircut.

"It's a little outta my way. And if I'm late, those Nelson brothers will dock my pay for the whole morning."

"That's not fair," Paige said.

"Did you say the Nelson brothers?" TJ asked.

"Yeah, Nelson Brothers' Bakery. That's where I work. We make Crispy Cruellers."

"Crispy Cruellers," TJ repeated. "Nelson Brothers' Crispy Cruellers."

"That's them. They taste great, but I wouldn't

know it anymore. I've worked there ten years and I've lost my appetite for them."

"What if I called them and got them not to dock your pay?"

Janice laughed.

"Sure. And why don't you ask them for a raise— and tell them the gals in the kitchens are so danged hot we need air-conditioning."

"Okay, I will. You'll get a raise."

Janice shook her head.

"You got style and charm even if you could use a job that pays enough to buy yourself some decent clothes. I'll drop you off at the Palmer House—right in front of that red carpet."

"You won't regret it," TJ said.

She shook her head.

"Tell me what else you'd like changed at your job," TJ prodded.

"Health insurance, for one. They got a lousy HMO that don't do . . ."

FOURTEEN

An hour later, the Ford Escort pulled to a stop in front of the Palmer House's red carpet. TJ got out and was immediately accosted by a uniformed doorman who asked him his business. TJ shouldered past him.

"Here, take this," Janice said, pulling a twenty out of her pocket and shoving it across the seat-back to Paige. "You'll need it."

"Oh, no, no," Paige said. "But thank you. Thank you for everything."

"I do it all the time. But no one's entertained me as much as your man telling me he's going to get me a raise and change my health insurance and set me up with a pension fund."

"He'll do it, too."

"Sure he will," Janice said. "You'd best catch up with him."

They squeezed each other's hand. As the Escort pulled away from the curb, Paige stepped into the revolving door. She pushed aside a second doorman's imperious questions.

"I'm with him," she said. She marched up the marble steps to the luxuriously appointed Palmer House lobby. TJ was at the front desk, a doorman hovering, prepared to muscle him out.

"I have a reservation," TJ insisted.

"We'd like some identification, sir," the desk clerk replied haughtily.

"I don't have my wallet."

"Then I'm afraid, sir, we cannot welcome you to this hotel. Perhaps you might consider the Pacific Gardens Mission House. It's for . . . transients such as yourself."

"Look, I'm TJ Skylar. I'm here for the SunOil meeting. I had a little, well, a little car trouble."

The desk clerk gave TJ the once-over. Twice. And then looked at Paige.

A lot of car trouble, he seemed to muse.

"Without any identification, sir, or without any means of payment for your room, we cannot . . ."

"Just call the president of SunOil. He's staying here as well."

"I will not disturb a guest at this early hour."

"Please," TJ said in a voice neither pleading nor arrogant. "I'm cold; I'm tired; I'm wet, and I'm late for the meeting of my life with Mr. Smith."

"Did I hear my name called?" A short, bald-headed gentleman in a gray suit stepped up to the desk. The suit was Italian cut and made of expensive silk, and yet did not quite fit his broad shoulders and the broader belly. "I just came down to get the morning's newspaper and all this commotion caught my attention!"

"Oh, Mr. Smith," the desk clerk said. "This . . . gentleman says he will be attending your . . ."

"TJ!" Mr. Smith roared. "You old coot, you look

like hell. What's with your shirt? You look like a young Marlon Brando."

He held his hand out to shake TJ's and then clearly thought the better of it. He regarded the desk clerk as he would a three-day-old fish.

"What did you say the problem was?"

"No problem, sir, I was checking in Mr. Skylar," the desk clerk said, attending to his keyboard. "Yes, Mr. Skylar, we have reserved for you a suite on the top floor which I think you will find acceptable."

"I had better go find my newspaper," Mr. Smith said. "I'll see you at the meeting. And I'll tell Shawna at breakfast that you're here. She'll be so relieved."

"About Shawna. I need to talk to you."

Mr. Smith held his palm up.

"Oh, heavens, not now, not now. Business first. Love—we'll talk about that later," he said and waddled toward the gift shop.

"But, Mr. Smith, I don't think you'll like what I have to say," TJ warned.

"I'm sure that if you two are happy, I will like it," Mr. Smith called over his shoulder.

"Mr. Skylar, if you could just sign here," the desk clerk said, leaning over the marble countertop. "And do you have any luggage?"

"No, but I do have a friend," TJ said, gesturing toward Paige.

The desk clerk sniffed.

"Well, then I can give you two keys."

"Separate beds?" Paige asked.

"There are two bedrooms to the suite," the desk clerk said.

"We won't be needing that many," TJ said, taking the keys from the clerk's hand and guiding Paige to the elevator.

"TJ, are you about to suggest something stupid? After all I've said?"

"I've been listening to you, sweetheart."

"How come I'm getting the impression that you haven't heard a word I've said?"

"I've heard you loud and clear. With all my senses. And not just your words."

"What do you mean?"

He touched her nose with the tip of his index finger.

"Darling, you want me."

She reared back.

"I do not!"

"Yes, you do. You want to make love to me right now. I can see it in your eyes. The way the green is getting greener."

"I do not want to make love to you. It would destroy a friendship."

He shook his head at her prim denial.

"No shame in it, darling. I want to make love to you, too."

"I never said—"

"Oh, you've said it. Said it with every move of your body."

He stepped into the elevator. Standing at the floor panel was a slim businesswoman carrying a designer handbag. She sniffed loudly and departed. Paige's head swiveled as she passed.

"What'd you say to her?"

The elevator doors slid shut.

"Nothing. It was my aura that got to her. The aura of a man who is going to get what he wants."

She allowed herself one glance at the mirrored wall. Was the green in her eyes really greener? Then she came face-to-face with him.

There was no mistaking his intentions. Her hand reached to close the gap of flesh and cotton at the neck of his shirt. But he stopped her with a kiss.

"It's too late for this," Paige whispered into his lips.

"Late is better than never," he said huskily. "And too late—well, Paige, it's never too late."

She shook her head and wormed out of his embrace.

"TJ, maybe I'd better just say goodbye now," she said. "I'll call my bank and ask them to wire me some money. And then I'm going."

He shrugged, as if her words were tiny fireflies, annoying but not of any concern.

"You can't walk out of here looking like that. Take a shower. The concierge is bringing up a change of clothes for each of us. Then if you want, you can go."

"Separate bedrooms?"

"Sure, but we're not going to need them."

"No, you're wrong. As soon as I clean up, I'm outta here."

"Sure you are, darlin'," he said, his voice as smooth as good whiskey.

The door opened with a hum of machinery and twelve celestial pings exhorting the elevator's occupants to exit on this, the twelfth floor.

In vain.

He figured this was his last chance.

Something about the tilt of her chin, something about the way her thoughts seemed to already have moved beyond him. He took her face into his hands.

"Paige, I have to do this. When I'm done, if you want to slap me and act indignant, go right ahead."

"I will. I absolutely will."

There were a hundred reasons she could have used to refute him. That he was too driven and could never have a relationship with a woman that took up more than its compartmentalized allowance. That she wanted something from life that wasn't going to be found in the city, wasn't going to be found in the boardroom, wasn't going to be found in a salary stub. That they had waited too long, becoming friends that shared an intimacy that precluded sexual love. That the friendship could be destroyed and it was a friendship more precious to her than any lover would or could be.

Or she could have told him, at long last, about her father. And the shame and agony that awaited her at what should be a simple high school reunion.

None of this she said. Instead, she looked up at him from beneath long, jet lashes. Still with some fight in her, resisting him to the very end. He brought his head down to her lips.

And kissed her. Definitely not a friendly kiss. Not a hello peck on the cheek. Not an air kiss behind the ear. No, he took the sweetness and newness that was her taste and he filled himself.

It was as intense as the first firecrackers on the Fourth of July. As magical as the first dusting of snow in winter. As quietly transforming as the drops of baptismal water on a baby's forehead.

She tried to call his name, but the word became a moan and the moan became a pleading for more. She was always his equal in friendship; and she was twenty-eight, for goodness' sakes, an age when some of her friends were working on second husbands or giving up on men entirely.

It was a glorious kiss, if you went in for having every nerve in your mouth, some you had never suspected you had, being brought to a dizzying crescendo of sensation.

It was a dizzyingly beautiful kiss, if you went in for turning your body into a screaming mass of nerve endings wanting more and more.

It was phenomenal kiss, if you wanted to be kissed within an inch of your life.

Containing a passion which, clearly, the woman who had exited the elevator did not wish to be confronted with.

"You people are disgusting!" she announced as the doors opened and a solo ping! announced that they were back on the first floor. She held her designer bag like a weapon ready to strike TJ. "Are you guests at this hotel?"

Her tomato-red lips pressed together disapprovingly as she waited for an answer. Paige self-consciously pulled at TJ's undershirt, trying to do the impossible—shield herself from the woman's righteous ire with his massive chest.

The shirt stretched taut against his muscles.

"Yes, we are," TJ replied.

The woman's mouth opened wide, revealing four

mercury-filled cavities and a little of her lipstick on her front tooth.

"Then you have a room key," she said at last. "Use it!"

TJ stepped in front of Paige and hit the twelfth-floor button again.

"Thanks for the suggestion. We're planning to do just that."

FIFTEEN

The elevator doors closed.

"Don't," he said gently, taking Paige's hand and uncurling her grip on the oxford cotton shirt. "I like looking at you. You know, friends don't look at each other enough. I rely on you. I talk to you. I watch stupid television shows with you. I go to movies with you. I take long walks with you. But, my God, Paige, I never spent enough time looking at you."

They were going to make love. She knew it from the way his eyes lingered hungrily on her body. He had never looked at her in just this way, a way that was both admiring and acquisitive. She knew if she stepped out of the elevator all the rationalizations, all the reasons, all the sense in being sensible would be left on the elevator's expensive parquet floor.

And yet, when the elevator's bells struck midnight, she was the Cinderella in reverse, coming into a ball of unimaginable beauty and riches. Leaving behind all thought, she let him lead her down the gold-carpeted hall to the gilt-paneled door.

The door opened into a spacious sitting room with a picture window overlooking the Loop. A green velvet couch with a carved mahogany frame was flanked by two needlepoint-cushioned chairs. A fireplace and low-slung coffee table completed the elegant setting.

On either side of the room were open doors leading to bedrooms. Separate bedrooms, just as the desk clerk had promised. The beds were both covered with ornately quilted gold cloth. A butler's tray in one corner of the sitting room tempted the hungry and weary with a bottle of fine French champagne, two Waterford flutes, a bowl of fresh fruit, a dozen pink roses in a white porcelain vase, and a leather-bound room service menu.

The luxurious surroundings made Paige self-conscious.

"Um, I'd better take a shower," she said. "I'm such a mess. I still have all that grit from the road. I haven't used antiperspirant. I haven't brushed my teeth in a day and a half—I'm surviving on breath mints."

"We're taking a shower together," TJ said and he shut one bedroom door decisively even as he took her hand to lead her to the other. "I'm not letting you out of my sight."

"TJ, you have a meeting in two—"

"Shhh. Let's forget all that. Haven't you ever heard of living for the moment?"

The look on his face was the boyish acknowledgment that she had taught him this life-lesson. But then as he tugged his shirt over her head, his expression grew serious.

"That mesh t-shirt is dangerous," he said. The t-shirt fluttered to the ground and he undid the beribboned clasp on her delicate leopard-print bra. For a moment, he stood in worshipful silence. He found himself kneeling, steadying himself with a hand against the small of her back. He pressed his face against her round, full breasts, feeling her stomach tighten. He realized his chin was rough and probably hurt her.

And yet, when he pulled away, she held him tight. The hot vanilla scent of her wanting made him hard. He stood up and took off his shirt. She touched his firm, hairless pectorals, glanced down modestly, and then with surprising boldness, met his eyes.

"We're dirty as all get-out," she said.

"I like it like that," he replied mischievously.

"A shower. Now."

"All right, darlin', I can wait. Question is, can you?"

He shucked off jeans and boots, even his briefs, and strode to the bathroom.

He hoped like hell that she was following.

"Coming, Paige?"

He glanced back. She was blushing. Goddamn, a real honest-to-goodness, five-alarm blush. Nice to see that on a woman for a change, instead of the smoldering cosmopolitan-gal challenges he got a lot of. But he wiped any satisfaction off his face when her lips pursed together tightly. Disapproval. Yup, that's usually what it meant when Paige's lips tightened.

Or fear. My goodness, she was afraid. Afraid of taking those clothes off.

She ducked her head and slowly, deliciously slowly, undid the button on her jeans. She pushed the waistband just below her hips, then shimmied as delectably as a showgirl until the denim hit the floor. At first, she tried to use her hands as some sort of modesty shield. One hand would cover what her panties didn't manage; the other would move along her chest. But petite as Paige was, her hands couldn't cover everything that a man would want to gander at.

She gave up. Dropped her hands to her side. And let him—no, dared him—to have a good, long, thirst-slaking look.

He hadn't looked at her, not much anyhow; friends never did. They took their friends' looks for granted, taking a week to notice a new haircut, longer to notice a different lipstick. But as a lover, Paige was a woman to look at, to savor, to admire.

She wasn't skinny as he remembered. Not to say she was fat, but she had a certain womanliness that came with age, if not with experience. Her breasts were round and if the hard nipples didn't tip skyward the way that some top models' did . . . well, that didn't make his fingers ache to touch them any less. Her stomach was flat and untried, in the way of a woman who has never been a mother. Her legs were long and had a slightly muscular appearance—Paige, after all, being as disciplined about hitting the treadmill as she was about hitting the books in college.

"Are you going to shower in your panties?" he asked.

She bit her lower lip so hard that it turned white. She was uncomfortable; but for some reason, he liked it. He knew he would make love to her, that he would have her as his own. And the more she protested indignation, by contrast, the more pleasurable the lovemaking.

She turned around, took three steps away. His heart lurched.

Damn, had he gone too far? Was she going to leave him standing here with an ache for her that was . . .

"Can you really wait?"

She tossed her head. Pulled her panties down, giving him a good long look at her rounded hips. And then she turned around, squared her shoulders, stared him down. The small triangle of pale, delicate hair at her womanhood was like a flame to heat.

"I can't wait," he said, crossing the floor in two quick strides.

She shook her head.

"Shower first. I thought you said I was the one who wouldn't be able to wait."

As she sauntered into the bathroom, he realized that for the first time with a woman, he wasn't sure who was in charge. When he followed, she was already in the tub, behind the mottled glass doors, rinsing her hair beneath a steaming jet of water. She turned her back on him when he entered. He picked up the bar of complimentary soap and tore off its wrapping.

He lathered up his hands and massaged her back and shoulders. Her skin was soft and smooth under his fingers. She put her hands up against the wall for balance. He soaped her arms for innocence, her rounded buttocks for pleasure, and the triangle of hair between her legs for reasons that had nothing to do with innocence. She groaned. He felt his confidence surge. He crouched down and massaged each leg, reveling in the curve of her calves, the tiny ankles. And then he rose, sliding his wet body against hers until the friction drove her wild. One hand he forced against the wall in front of Paige so that he could ensure she didn't fall; the other hand pleasured her—and by doing so, him—with slow, soapy caresses of her breasts, her stomach, and then the thatch of hair that enclosed her womanhood, moist but not with water.

She arched, rearing back so hard that he nearly lost his balance.

"Do you want to wait until we get into bed?" he asked huskily.

"I guess I'm not as strong as I thought I was."

"No, darling, you're strong. But in a woman's way."

His hardness strained against her pelvis and she stood on her toes so that he could enter her. With one hand he held them both up to the warm waterfall. His other hand came around to her front, sluicing the water from her stomach, pausing at the triangle of hair, and then touching the delicate nub of pleasuring flesh. Her head fell back against his shoulder, damp curls matting against his chest.

She moaned once, called to him, but he was past hearing her. As the first violent contractions of her climax began, she reached back to urge him on. Reflexively, he unclenched. His self-control faltered and gave way. One touch brought him to orgasm. He felt his own pulsing mixed with her name.

The name of a lover.

* * *

He washed her hair afterwards, feeling a wistfulness at his own immaturity.

"How come I never noticed how sexy you are?"

"I don't know," she said, blushing pink all the way down to her toes.

"Let's go to bed. Jump on the mattresses. See if this deluxe hotel has one of those vibrating massage machines that we can waste our quarters on."

"Not yet."

She offered him a thick, plush robe with the Palmer House crest on the pockets. He didn't take it. She put it on.

"Play time's over," she said. "You have a meeting to go to."

He growled but reluctantly pulled a towel around his waist. Paige fixed her hair with a plastic comb she found in a basket of toiletries left for guests. TJ started to shave, holding the plastic disposable razor up to his cheek as he stared in the mirror.

Paige would simply have to come back to New York, he concluded. She'd come to her senses. All she had needed to make her life complete was to have him not just as a friend, but as everything—lover and husband.

The word husband stopped him short. Husband. He leaned forward, regarding himself in the mirror speculatively. The scruffy beard didn't fit his image of a husband. And that would be the next step in this relationship. Marriage.

How could he have ever thought he'd be happy, or at least content, with Shawna?

"Here, let me," Paige said, coming up behind him

to take the razor. She gently lathered up his face and drew the blade across his cheek. "You want to look good for your meeting, don't you?"

The hotel bathrobe should have been as enticing as, well, a bathrobe.

But a single droplet of water ran down her neck, waiting to be licked . . .

"TJ, your meeting!"

"What meeting? Oh, that meeting."

"You've got just half an hour," she said. "Hold still, I've left a mustache."

He thought of the ring, the three—or was it five?—carat diamond in the box in the sitting room.

"Paige, I've got something to tell you. Something I planned to do but which I know I'm not going to follow through on."

"Don't talk. I'm going to nick you."

He took the razor out of her hand and kissed her. He left a tiny dot of shaving cream on her cheek.

"It doesn't affect us now, but you should know about it."

"Is this a relationship talk?"

"Yeah, I guess it is."

"I thought the woman was supposed to ask *where is this relationship going?*"

"Glad you asked. I think there's only one thing we can do now."

She took the razor.

"Shhhh. I can't shave you when you're talking. Nothing's changed. Besides, you've got this meeting with the Motorcon and SunOil people."

He took the razor out of her hand and kissed her. Long, slow, and wet.

"I've got more important things to do besides go to meetings."

SIXTEEN

As he drew her out of the bathroom, there was a firm-but-quiet rapping on the suite's door.

"Who is it?" TJ asked.

"Concierge," a voice replied. "I have for your approval, sir, a size 44-long suit, a selection of dress shirts and ties, socks, underwear, and a selection of ladies' apparel."

TJ put a finger to Paige's lips and stripped her of the bathrobe.

"Wha—"

"Keep the bed warm for me," he said with a wink.

Closing the bedroom door on her luscious outrage, he put on the robe and let in the concierge, who wore the gold-trimmed navy uniform of the Palmer House. True to his word, the hotel official in charge of guest comforts had thought of everything.

Right down to a new bra-and-pantie set in a pink-and-gold shopping bag.

"Will that be all, sir?"

TJ picked up his dirty jeans, the oxford shirt, Paige's jeans, her mesh shirt. He decided he couldn't give up the mesh shirt.

He put it in his bathrobe pocket. After all, it was

a souvenir. And besides, he didn't like the idea of this concierge in a monkey suit touching it.

The concierge eyed the leopard-print bra and matching panties forming a path to the bedroom. TJ kicked them under the sofa.

He gave the laundry to the concierge, plucking out from the jeans pocket the small velvet jeweler's box and the bill Officer Kerner had given him. He held out the twenty.

"Thank you, sir," the concierge said, folding his tip into his uniform's breast pocket. "I shall have these cleaned immediately."

"Not too immediately," TJ muttered as he shut the door. He opened the box, inspected the diamond ring, and put the box on the butler's tray.

He reentered the bedroom. Paige stood beside the window wearing another robe. Bad sign, the robe.

Would have been better if she had been waiting beneath the sheets.

"I think we should get dressed."

"Nah," he said lazily, grabbing her hand and, in one smooth motion, bringing her into bed beneath his strong, muscular body.

Knock, knock.

"TJ, I think it's the concierge again."

"They can't clean our clothes in an hour. Too much mud. Grease. Dirt. Sweat."

Knock, knock. More aggressive. Demanding a reply. Knock, knock.

"I'm sure I heard the door."

"Okay, okay, but we don't even need those clothes. We got new ones."

"Maybe it's the folks from SunOil."

He wrinkled his nose. He wasn't looking forward to any of the morning's necessary work.

Knock, knock.

"All right! I'm coming," he said impatiently, thinking that the concierge was a mite too efficient, a fraction too good at his job.

He rose from the bed, smiling at Paige's frank admiration of his body.

"Don't move," he warned.

He put on his robe, crossed the sitting room, and opened the door.

In all his nightmares, in all his darkest hours, TJ would never have envisioned opening the door to the stunning platinum-blonde titan in a tight red lycra dress.

The same beauty who graced calendars, posters, magazine advertisements, and coffee mugs.

"Hello, darling!" she gushed, throwing her arms around him. "Daddy told me the jeweler called him to say you'd been in. You were going to surprise me with a wedding proposal—oh, darling, of course I'll say *yes*. I think we'll make a dynamite team!"

Sensing some resistance, she pulled away.

"Oh, dear," she said, her bubble gum-pink lips drooping to a pout. "Now you're mad at me for spoiling the surprise."

Shawna glanced beyond his shoulder. Her eyes met those of Paige. Who stood in the doorway wrapped in a Palmer House bathrobe and a hurt expression.

"I guess we're all surprised," Paige observed.

"Shawna, we need to talk," TJ said as the gorgeous blonde swept past him into the sitting room. "But now's not a good time."

"Good morning, Paige," Shawna said.

Paige was silent. TJ rubbed a headache that was beginning at his forehead and working its way through his whole skull.

"Shawna, I'm sorry that you had to find out this way . . . hey, put that down."

"Five carats," Shawna said, picking up the jeweler's box on the butler's tray. She held it out for Paige's inspection. "A brilliant diamond in a brilliant setting, wouldn't you agree?"

Paige peered at the glittering jewel. Both women turned to look at TJ. Neither looked happy with him.

"Which one of us gets this?" Shawna asked. "I mean, I don't mind sharing a man but I don't want to share a business."

"You don't have to share him," Paige said. "He's all yours."

His mouth went dry.

"No, Paige, please don't."

"Most men don't walk around with five-carat diamonds in their pockets," Paige said.

"There was a reason."

"I don't care what the reason is."

"Yeah, you do," he countered, desperate now.

"Oh, really?" she asked.

TJ knew a lot of men in his shoes would lie. Or worse, offer no explanation at all. But both women deserved the truth from him.

"Paige, I thought part of this trip to Chicago was that I was going to ask Shawna to marry me."

"You still can," both women said, with varying degrees of hostility.

Shawna perched on the couch, opening a chocolate from the complimentary basket. She sniffed it and was poised to lob the treat into the wastebasket under the desk. The Oil-Me-Up Girl couldn't afford the calories, which might translate to an extra centimeter of flesh in the next calendar or magazine ad.

But this was an emergency. Shawna popped the chocolate into her mouth and then picked out another. And another.

Meanwhile, Paige grabbed the first article of clothing she could find that wasn't 44-long. A dress, a black jersey knit and a little big in the shoulders—great for a funeral, which this party was quickly becoming. She shrugged it over her head as she deftly maneuvered out of her bathrobe—not an inch more skin showed than when she wore her most conservative business suit. Then she plunged her hand into the shopping bag from the lingerie shop, coming up with panties and a bra. She pulled the panties up under her dress. The tags scratched her stomach, but she didn't care.

She accomplished this while the Oil-Me-Up Girl ate three more chocolates and TJ sputtered a useless apology.

"Paige, please don't go. What we have is special And I don't want to lose it."

"Yes, we have a special friendship," she said, emphasizing the word *friendship*. "But it should have stayed just that and nothing more. Sorry, Shawna, this looks bad. But whatever it was, it isn't anymore. At all. You can have him."

She shoved her feet into her wet, dirty sneakers and snagged her keys from the wrapper-littered coffee table.

"Paige, don't . . ."

She paused at the door just as the concierge reappeared holding a stack of clean, lavender-scented clothes. Paige took her jeans and the zip-lock bag he produced in which her temporary driver's license, soggy but still readable, was sealed.

"Paige, I'm sorry I didn't tell you about marrying Shawna," TJ said, following Paige out into the hallway. "You know that I had been thinking that I should settle down. Shawna and I thought we were good for each other because we're both devoted to business. You know we've been going out off and on for three years, ever since her father came to me with the SunOil problems, and—"

"Puh-leeze, I always told you that I'd much rather be your friend in ten years than your lover," Paige said. "A friendship is more valuable, more lasting and enduring. I hope I can be your friend . . . someday. A long time from now. After I stop being riproaring mad at you. For now, maybe you'd better talk to your fiancee."

"She's not my fiancee. Where are you going?"

He followed her to the elevator bank.

"To my high school reunion," she said, punching the down button. "And don't do something silly like follow me—not that you'd ever step foot in Sugar Mountain again. But don't make a fool out of yourself. Go back to that room."

"Paige, I'm already a fool. I wanted to make love to you because you told me that making love changed your mind about a lot of things. I wanted to change your mind. About your life. About New York. About me."

"Oh, you've changed my mind all right. I now think you're a jerk. I didn't used to."

"Because I didn't tell you about Shawna? But I'm not going to marry her."

"Here's why I'm mad," Paige said, holding up two fingers. "Number one, you didn't think I was a good-enough friend to tell me you were *thinking* of marrying her."

"Yeah, but—"

He couldn't finish his sentence.

"I didn't tell you I quit my job because I was afraid you would talk me out of it. And you didn't tell me you were thinking of getting married. Because, well, I don't know why. But either way, we must not be very good friends if we didn't want to tell each other the most important things."

"I didn't tell you because I thought you'd disapprove."

"Sure, I disapprove because you don't love her. But that wasn't stopping you from marrying her. No. I was never really your friend, was I?"

"We are friends. Best friends. Maybe I wanted more, something different, something special between us. Like what we had just now. I just didn't know it. What would be wrong about that? Maybe we could start over."

"It's too late for that. I don't respect you anymore."

"Why?"

"Because you cheated on her. That's reason number two."

"On Shawna? But we've never had that kind of relationship. You know that. We went out with other people all the . . ." He shut up. He had done wrong. He knew it. He bowed his head. "I'm sorry, Paige."

"Don't apologize to me. Go apologize to her," Paige ordered. "And by the way, congratulations if you are getting married. And tell Shawna, I'm really, really sorry, too. I don't deserve her forgiveness. But I had no damn idea she was going down the aisle with you."

She punched the elevator button and the doors closed on his anguished face.

SEVENTEEN

He stood for several seconds, paralyzed.

The concierge coughed discreetly at his shoulder.

"Will that be all, sir?"

"Yeah, sure."

The concierge didn't move.

"Here," Shawna said, pulling out a twenty-dollar bill from her handbag. "Send up a pot of hot coffee. This man is late for an important meeting. The most important meeting of either one of our lives. Snap to it!"

"With pleasure, madam," the concierge said. He nodded at TJ as he passed by him, trotting down the hall and disappearing into an unmarked door as if he were a character in *Alice in Wonderland.*

"Shawna, I'm sorry," TJ said. "But I have to follow her."

"You might try getting dressed first."

He looked down at his bathrobe.

"Come on back in the room."

He followed her; but when the door closed behind them and he realized he was alone with her, he shook his head decisively.

"Shawna, I can't stay."

"You can't go without clothes on."

He grabbed his jeans from the pile of clothes the concierge had left. He considered where to change, an odd notion for him since he ordinarily was given neither to modesty nor exhibitionism.

Shawna closed the sitting room door and sat on the tufted leather bench by the window. She parted the curtains with a hand and appeared to be engrossed in the passing scenery.

TJ shoved his feet into his jeans.

"TJ, you're not going anywhere. Except downstairs. She said *jerk* and she meant it. And besides, you have a meeting. My father's people are waiting."

"I don't want to go," he said, pulling apart the cellophane wrapping on a button-down shirt.

"If you don't go, you will have failed my father, his company, and everyone who works for him. Don't fail them now, TJ; they're hanging by a thread. If we don't turn SunOil around and take Motorcon with us, it's economic failure."

Failure.

A fleeting image came to him, an image that he pushed away so often, but an image that affected everything he did, everything he was.

Ten years ago, Sugar Mountain was colder than in memory. The snows were deep, compacted and recompacted from storms that blew in from the Pacific Northwest with furious winds. The Skylar matriarch had said no when the boys wanted to go up, but TJ and Jack were home from college for the holidays and they were itching to go. The two younger ones understood a challenge and nothing was going to keep them from the mountain.

They started early, checked their equipment, and

kept up a steady-but-slow pace. The mountains were home, every rock and every crevice familiar to them—and yet, this year was different. Blame it on snow, blame it on winds, blame it on some shift in the hemisphere that the Skylar brothers had failed to notice. There were slipups, some missed markers.

But TJ wouldn't turn back if Jack didn't. And Jack didn't want to turn back until he had conquered again the mountain he so loved.

Then Jack lost his footing. Rappeling down with pebbles dropping into nothingness, Jack dropped on the precipice. Hanging by a single hand, the other hand snagged in his line. TJ ordered their younger brother Win to go for help—dangerous enough in itself because it meant a climb alone. TJ cautiously positioned himself over Jack, grabbing his hand and pulling hard. But the lines were tugging Jack down—down into hundreds of feet of nothingness. TJ would have hung on forever, even with his fingers numb and an icicle made of his tears frozen to his cheek. Matt grabbed him by the waist and hung on.

Still, he lost purchase. A slip of an inch. And then a foot. Matt tried to hang on to TJ, but his grip was weakening. And then TJ felt Jack's hand go limp.

"Let go," Jack urged. "I'm going to take you down and Matt besides."

"Can't let go," TJ screamed over the wind. "You go, we all go."

The Skylar motto. The boys never climbed alone. Never hiked in the summer without all of them going. When the youngest one had barely a single hair on his chin, they all went in the pickup truck on Saturday nights, down to Vail, to check out the girls.

Their chivalrous code demanded that if Jack got himself a girl, TJ had to have one and so did Win and Matt. 'Course, that meant that they didn't get girls often—though some girls got wise and brought along their kid sisters when they cruised the drag.

You go, we all go.

TJ glanced back at Matt, whose face was white with fear.

"Hang on to me," he ordered.

"I am; just keep holda Jack."

TJ looked down at the snow. He wasn't losing ground; he was losing Jack . . . centimeter by centimeter. His hand was so damn slippery . . . and Jack twisting.

"TJ, it's beautiful, isn't it?"

And for an instant TJ had looked up to see what Jack saw—the delicately frosted rooftops and the shivering pines of Sugar Mountain, icicles glittering in the sun.

"No, Jack, no!"

An empty hand, cold and red and wet.

"No?" Shawna asked softly, bringing him back to the present. She stood up. *"No* is not an option, sweetheart. Failure is not an option."

Failure. The image was gone. The emptiness left by his brother's death carved its relentless place in his ribs.

He unflexed his hand and looked at Shawna. She smiled gently.

"I can forgive," she said. "I can even forget. But you'd never forgive yourself and I'd never forget if you let my father down this morning."

He closed his eyes.

"If men and women can ever be friends, you have to let her go now. You give her time and then you apologize."

"And if I want more?"

"I don't think she wants more. She would have stayed. But you owe me, TJ; you owe me this meeting. It's the most important thing in the world to me, SunOil. I won't lose it."

"All right," he said, sighing wearily. "Get me some coffee, please."

"That's better."

TJ shaved off his mustache in the bathroom and dressed in the suit she laid out for him on the untouched bed in the other bedroom. She gave him a cup of coffee and a doughnut he couldn't manage. Just before he stood up to leave, she put the jeweler's box in his shirt pocket.

"We won't do anything about this right now," she said. "We'll talk about it later."

"Shawna, I don't think I can—"

She put her finger on his lips.

"Let's not talk about it now. We have so much to do this morning. And I don't want either one of us to say anything hurtful. We've never had a grand passion between us, but we do have respect. I don't get that from a lot of men and I like it in you. Let's not ruin that."

He followed her to the elevator and tallied up his weary hours. But when he heard the single desultory *ping,* he strode out of the elevator with an appearance of confidence and control. Shawna stepped behind him.

They entered a large conference room with a

twelve-man table. TJ endured a hearty hello and a backslapping hug from Shawna's father and shook hands with the president of Motorcon. Then he took his place at the head of the table.

Shawna signed an autograph for one of the tax accountants, who didn't seem to mind at all the view of her breasts as she bent over the notepad. Then she discreetly sat on a chair by the window, tugging her skirt as far down as it would go.

"No, Shawna, come on up here," TJ suggested. "There's a seat here, right by me."

The men jogged each other's elbows. Shawna's father leaned across the table and whispered that there was an engagement to announce. TJ winced.

"She's got no interest in business," Mr. Smith said. "We'd just bore her."

Shawna didn't move a muscle.

"All right, fine," TJ conceded. "Let's talk merger between the two best American producers of cutting-edge automotive technology."

The words *best* and *cutting edge* hadn't been applied to either saggy stock-priced company in a long time, so a gentle murmur of approval warmed the table and the men concentrated on the notebooks which had been prepared for them by TJ's company.

"We will begin, gentlemen, by turning to page three," TJ said. "Page . . . Paige . . ."

He had had friendships with men fall apart. Drifting apart because of marriages, company transfers, or something as simple as not getting season tickets together.

Sometimes friendships ended with an explosive bang. TJ had recently broken off relations with a longtime friend when he had discovered the man had "churned," recommending stock purchases to clients for the sole purpose of increasing his commissions.

Other times friendships ended in a whimper of missed phone calls, unanswered E-mails, and Christmas cards marked return to sender, addressee unknown.

TJ knew he was unusual among his male colleagues in the attention he paid to friendship. But he had little in the way of family.

His mother had all but cut off contact with him after Jack's death. His secretary sent flowers at all the major holidays, but she had never seen fit to forgive him and he had never seen fit to ask for forgiveness, burying his guilt and fears. His youngest brother, Win, had skipped out of Sugar Mountain, and no one knew where he was. His other brother, Matt, claimed to be too busy to fly into New York, no matter how many times TJ sent tickets.

Every friend was as precious to TJ as diamonds—but none more so than Paige.

"Paige, Paige, Paige . . ."

"TJ, darling, do you want us to look at the price earnings graph on page three?" Shawna said, slipping into the seat beside him.

"Sure," he said absently. "The price earnings . . . page."

At three o'clock, the men were jovial, best of friends really. Even the accountants popped champagne corks and talked about the good times a-comin'. TJ disengaged himself from the group. Tired. So damn tired.

"We'll talk after you get some shut-eye," Shawna said, slipping into the elevator with him. "Don't worry, I won't jump you. No, no, don't talk. Just let's go upstairs. You look like somebody hit you over the head with a steel tire iron."

"That's how I feel," TJ conceded. "And I'm not good company."

"I'm not company. I want your briefcase. You sleep and let me do some reading."

He left her in the sitting room. Shawna had slipped off her heels and curled up with the papers his office had faxed over. She could have them. He just wanted to sleep. He tugged his tie loose, shrugged off his suit jacket, and kicked off his shoes. When he hit the bed, he was sure he would fall right to sleep.

And he almost did, but not before noticing that Paige's scent, fresh and clean, was still on the sheets. And it had become a very *un*-innocent vanilla perfume.

Wearily, wearily, he fell into a dream. A familiar one. He was in church. Waiting for his bride. No, no, waiting for his best man. Where was Paige? Surrounding him at the altar were his brothers—surprising that Jack was there. He still hadn't gotten a haircut.

"Hey, it's a dream," Jack explained. "I get to be here. If you want."

"Of course I want you to be here. You're my brother. But where's my best man?"

"I'll be your best man."

"No, if it's okay with you, I've got someone else in mind. Paige."

"I'll take over since she isn't here. Your bride's

walking up the aisle and you don't have time to go looking for Paige."

"But she's my best man."

"It's a dream, buddy. She'll get here if you want her to."

I want her to; I want her to, TJ thought as he watched the veiled bride approach on the arm of a beaming Mr. Smith. *I want her to, I want her to.* But no Paige appeared at the end of the aisle or at his shoulder. But her scent was on his mind, so tantalizing he was almost certain she was near him. But he just couldn't see her.

"Such a beautiful wedding," Mr. Smith said to him as he relinquished his daughter's arm to TJ. "I know you two will be so very happy. Now that you're a success."

He glanced over his bride's shoulder to see if maybe Paige had slipped into the back of the church.

Then he looked at Shawna. Her veil was so damned frothy and white.

He was marrying Shawna, wasn't he? After all, that's what he had agreed to do. He searched the back of the church and saw Shawna. She waved to him, wistfully, and walked through the doors into a brilliant light.

Puzzled, TJ looked at his bride. If she weren't Shawna, just who the heck was . . .

He raised her veil.

"Hi, Paige," he said, relieved to see her. "I'm so glad you came back."

"I didn't come back, you silly. I've been here all along."

* * *

He bolted upright, wide awake.

He wasn't in church. He was in Chicago.

He wasn't with Paige. He had Shawna out in the sitting room, reading his papers.

He wasn't a success. He was a failure because he had ruined a wonderful friendship.

But men and women couldn't be friends. Or at least, he couldn't be friends with Paige. He couldn't be just friends. No, he loved her, truly loved her too much for just friends.

He had thought making love would change her, but it was he who had been changed. With just one touch.

Feeling oddly confident given what he was about to do, he stepped out into the sitting room. Shawna looked up from her paperwork.

"I'm confused about clause b, slash one," she said. "Doesn't that unfairly give the Motorcon shareholders a percentage of before-tax profit . . . hey, stop a sec. Let me get my shoes. Where are you taking me?"

"Where you belong."

EIGHTEEN

"A woman CEO?" The president of Motorcon recoiled at the notion. "I don't get it. Is it a publicity stunt or something?"

"No, an honest-to-God CEO," TJ said. "The full-time SunOil CEO with a great love for the company and the industry. A CEO who just happens to be a woman."

"Yeah, but we're not talking about just any woman," the president pointed out.

The accountant rubbed his forehead with his palm. The vice presidents of Motorcon scratched their bald heads in unison. Mr. Smith registered his disbelief with shaking jowls and a wide-eyed stare.

"He's right. You're not just talking about the difference between an executive who puts on panty hose instead of black crew socks. You're talking about Shawna. My daughter. A beautiful girl. But just that—a beautiful girl."

"Thank you, Daddy," Shawna said, rising up on the toes of her already impossibly tall high heels to peer over TJ's shoulder.

"Yeah, a beauty who's the Oil-Me-Up Gal," Motorcon's president chimed in. "Customers won't like her as a CEO. They think of her as a sex goddess. Not a businesswoman."

His vice presidents shook their heads. *No, indeed,* they silently agreed. A sex goddess. That was what Shawna was. The world wasn't ready for Shawna Smith becoming a businesswoman.

"We can't sell out our employees to a company that's going to nose-dive on the NASDAQ exchange because you want to put a dame in the driver's seat. Besides," Motorcon's president drawled. He looked up at Shawna's—well, he aimed for her chin but faltered in his efforts about six inches shy. "No disrespecting you, Miss Smith, but you've got more corporate assets in your chassis than between your ears."

"Are you saying my daughter's stupid?" Mr. Smith challenged from across the table.

"No, no, of course not," the president said. His vice presidents shook their heads—perish the thought. "She's not stupid. It's just she's better as a corporate, uh, figure, figure, figure . . . uh, what's the word I'm looking for?"

"Figurehead," one of the vice presidents prompted.

His two fellow vice presidents nodded, make it three when the third's ribs were hit by a colleague's sharp elbow. The accountant took off his glasses and wiped the fogged lenses with his tie.

"Help me out here, gentlemen. Why exactly isn't Mr. Skylar going to take the job?" he asked. "I understood that he wasn't leaving his position at his brokerage house in New York but that he would oversee the SunOil financial package in a consultant capacity. At a considerable fee. Why won't you be doing that, Mr. Skylar?"

"Are you backing out on me, TJ?" Mr. Smith asked.

"I've got personal reasons," TJ explained. "And besides, I happen to think that Shawna would do a much better job than I would."

A collective gasp.

"The reorganization of the two companies was predicated on a strong executive officer," the accountant pointed out. He put on his glasses. "Someone who can make tough decisions about the unprofitable and weak links in our corporate chain. We're both running losing operations, and combining the companies was supposed to make us both stronger. Turn the red ink to black. That leader was supposed to be you, Mr. Skylar. I don't think stockholders are going to keep their money and their faith in us if we put a pinup girl in the executive suite."

"Don't fail us now," Mr. Smith said quietly.

"It's not a matter of failure," Shawna said.

She looked up at TJ, touched his cheek with wistful tenderness, and then hardened her jaw. She sat down. Not at the window seat. Not at the side of the table. And she didn't clasp her hands on the nape of her neck the way she did for the months of January, February, May, August, and October.

No, no, the Oil-Me-Up Girl sat down at the head of the conference table and tapped her vermilion-polished nails on the mahogany surface to get their attention. As if anything short of a car backfire in the hall could have distracted them.

"I would propose we begin with the Northwestern

Division of Motorcon," she said, and she directed a steady gaze at Motorcon's president. "Sir, you've been posting losses at thirteen-and-a-quarter off estimates for two years. A five percent cut in operating expenses across the board and the elimination of the South Dakota plant should bring those numbers up."

"But, but, but . . ." blubbered one of the vice presidents.

"Shaddup, your boss is talking," the accountant said with uncharacteristic courage. "Go on—Ms. Smith."

No one, but no one, had ever called the Oil-Me-Up Girl *Ms*.

She rewarded the accountant with a smile that was meant to be all business, but which, purely out of habit, was mega-watt sexually charged. The accountant reared up his shoulders and gulped, Adam's apple jogging furiously against his heavy-on-the-starch white collar. He'd have to work on controlling his blush—especially if he were going to make her his own.

Which he fully intended, now that he knew that there was a kindred number-crunching soul lurking in that body made for sin.

"I've asked Ms. Smith to reconsider the terms which require that Motorcon executives retire early," TJ said. "As a very wise man once told me, it's like making a man go to his own funeral."

"I agree," the president of Motorcon said. "But are you suggesting that we work for SunOil? For the Oil-Me-Up Girl . . . I mean, Shawna . . . I mean, Ms. Smith?"

"Absolutely," TJ said.

"Shawna, is this what you really want to do?" Mr. Smith asked, eyes narrowed. "I thought you enjoyed modeling."

Shawna glanced at TJ for courage.

"Quite frankly, I've always hated modeling. But I did it because it was good for the company. And that's what I care about. This company is my birthright."

"And what about TJ?"

"TJ? Oh, he's wonderful. But it wasn't meant to be. He wants to marry for love. And we don't love each other."

I do? TJ thought. He thought of Paige. Marriage? Love? At the end of friendship, maybe that was what there was. *Yeah, I guess I do want to marry. For love.*

I will marry for love, too, the accountant at the end of the table thought, adjusting his tie. He shook his head at the irony. Who would have thought that a beautiful mind lurked in that killer body?

Marry for love? Absolutely! the accountant resolved. Just had to be sure to do it after the first of the year to avoid the marriage penalty on jointly filed federal income tax returns.

The president of Motorcon, his minions, and Mr. Smith slumped into their seats, staring at the poster-girl-turned-tycoon.

"I'll be going now," TJ said as Shawna outlined her plan to streamline operations in the northwestern branches of the two companies.

Shawna gave him one of her man-melts-in-the-knees smiles, but it didn't have that effect on him today. Not another soul acknowledged his departure.

They were mesmerized. Ms. Smith might actually make all of them a heckuva lot of money—and that was always a surefire way to get a man's attention.

"I don't see a Paige Burleson," the concierge said. His dour face was illuminated by the turquoise glow of his computer screen. "I can assure you that she hasn't rented a car in Chicago."

"What about airline tickets?" TJ asked. "She would be heading for Colorado."

The concierge tapped a series of commands and waited for the computer to respond.

"Ms. Burleson didn't purchase a plane ticket at either Midway or O'Hare airport."

"Bus?"

The concierge pursed his lips and made a quick phone call.

"There are no buses leaving for Colorado from the Greyhound station," he said. "And the ticket master knows of no woman matching your friend's description who has arrived at the station within the past several hours."

"Amtrak?"

Another phone call.

"Sorry, sir. There are no westbound trains today."

"Could she hitchhike?" he asked, horrified at the prospect of her putting herself in danger that way.

"I shall ask the cab companies to radio their drivers with her description. If they make a sweep of the major arteries, we might be able to find her. But, sir? This may take some time. And more of those dead presidents. Not for myself, mind you, but for the search party."

TJ laid an envelope on the concierge's desk.

"Very good, sir. If you would like to have a seat in the lobby, I can have a waiter sent by with some light refreshments."

A half hour later, as TJ was signing for his replacement credit card at a green velvet couch in the center of the lobby, the concierge delivered his news.

"Sir, your Paige Burleson was not on any major thoroughfare in Chicago; nor has she entered a cab in the metropolitan area. If I may offer a suggestion, sir?"

"Yes?"

"It is extremely difficult to juggle two or more women. The blonde was awfully familiar—isn't she the Oil-Me-Up Girl?"

"No, as a matter of fact she's the CEO of the SunOil company."

The concierge received the correction with a sniff.

"Quite so. In any event, you prefer the brunette, perhaps?"

"She's my friend. My best friend."

The concierge sighed.

"Sir, it is a truism universally acknowledged and well worth repeating—men and women can never be friends. Men are complex creatures with needs, desires, and ambitions. Women have only one thing on their minds."

"And what would that one thing be?"

"I could scarcely say. I'm not a woman," the concierge said haughtily. "May I make arrangements for a rental car or perhaps a plane ticket? New York, Colorado, the West Coast?"

No way around it, he'd have to go home. Home to Sugar Mountain. The place he had carefully avoided. The place he feared when he had no fears. The place of failure, of his darkest hour.

"A plane ticket," he agreed reluctantly. "Denver, please."

"Very good, sir."

It was at that moment, as he looked up to acknowledge the concierge's unctuous bow, that he noticed a man in a Motorcon coverall crossing the Palmer House's large and opulently appointed lobby.

The man was in a hurry, didn't turn around, so TJ didn't see his face. But the thick, sunburnt back of his neck was familiar, as were the baseball cap and the dainty handkerchief that peeked out of the coverall back pocket.

It was embroidered with the initial *H*.

"Herman!" TJ shouted, upsetting the tray, his newspaper, and the concierge's equilibrium as he dashed across the lobby.

"Men are trouble, through and through," Janice said, popping her gum. She threw toll change into the bucket and shoved her foot down hard on the accelerator. "Take my first husband. Or even my second."

Please, Paige thought.

"Men and women cannot be friends," Janice said authoritatively. "Because women are complex creatures with needs, desires, and ambitions. Men, well, they have only one thing on their minds."

"He never had it on his mind. Not about me, at any rate."

"Ever?"

"Well, twice." And then, before Janice concluded a jog of her head that was meant as a substitute for the words *see? I told you so,* Paige added, "Twice in a friendship."

"And you?"

"I must have been fooling myself all this time. I must have always wanted more. And never knew it. Because when he touched me . . ."

"Don't have to say any more. I understand. And that's rough, girl."

"The roughest part is that I don't know that I'll ever be able to love another man," Paige said. "I'll always be measuring a man by TJ, and other men will always come up short. Even if he was a jerk."

Janice shook her head mournfully.

"That must be my problem. Every man I've ever met I've compared to John Travolta, and Johnny is one powerful good-looking man."

"You were John Travolta's friend?"

"No, but I've seen all his movies. And that's been enough to ruin me for any other man. And John Travolta's a jerk. I don't know that for certain, but I'm sure it must be true."

Paige bit her lip to keep herself from crying. Or laughing.

Janice dropped her off at the Middlefork Pound.

"Keep your money," she said when Paige pulled

out an envelope of cash which had been wired to the Palmer House by her secretary Nelly.

"But I owe you—"

"You owe me nothing," Janice said. "That friend of yours got me a raise and, best of all, Mr. Nelson said he'll take a look at getting us some decent insurance."

Janice sped off and Paige looked at the cars in the lot.

Well, the single solitary car in the lot. Middlefork was a small, law-abiding town.

"Help you, miss?" the attendant asked. He sat on a metal folding chair reading a week-old news magazine.

"Yeah, that one's mine."

"Title?"

"Here," she said. She pulled out the piece of paper that Herman had delivered to the Palmer House.

The attendant glanced at it.

"Fifty bucks."

She pulled out two twenties and a ten.

The attendant gave her the keys without looking up at her weary face.

The huge yellow Mustang was parked facing the sidewalk.

Its headlights drooped sympathetically as she approached.

"Take me home," Paige told it.

NINETEEN

Sugar Mountain was a great town to leave.

Great for growing up, safe and secure, sheltered from the troubles of a harsh and sophisticated world.

Its elementary school principal, descended from the school's nineteenth-century founder, still demanded respect, discipline, and a strict ban on gum-chewing. Her husband, who was the high school's principal and orchestral director, was known to disapprove of *Cliffs Notes,* rap music, and failure to remove one's baseball cap or football helmet during the national anthem.

Store owners kept house accounts on which kids could buy snacks on their way home from school. The library didn't bother to issue library cards—everyone signed out the books they needed on a sheet in the foyer. Doors were left unlocked unless someone went on vacation. The drugstore kept a jar by the stack of newspapers so people could just pay for the *Sugar Mountain Chronicle* without having to go through the checkout line.

Police and Fire Chief Matt Skylar possessed a phenomenal ability to remember children's full names and an even more amazing way of saying *whatcha up to?* so as to cause the most rambunctious youth to reconsider planned misbehavior. Matt had learned that talent from his predecessor, Police and Fire Chief Jeanne Schoder, who had used this ability to great effect on all nine of her children.

Mayor Stern organized a Fourth of July parade that usually generated more participants than spectators and an August Concert in the Park series that called upon Sugar Mountain's most enthusiastic, if not talented, musicians and orators.

A quiet place, a gentle place, a calming place. The kind of place where mothers shooed their children out the door on summer mornings with the admonition to "go find someone to play with." A place where shopkeepers would have scoffed at the suggestion to put in video cameras and strategically placed mirrors so that they could keep an eye on their customers. A place where everyone knew which neighbor needed help with their snow-shoveling, their lawn-mowing, and picking up groceries—and did it.

But not the sort of place for ambitious, itchin'-to-do-something-with-life, gotta-get-outta-here teens. Since most teens are of that nature, Sugar Mountain lost most of its high school graduates to college, to jobs in more cosmopolitan locales, and to the Armed Forces.

But Mayor Stern was a keen observer of human nature. He knew that humans, like many other animals, will someday tire of travel and will desire to return home. And when former citizens of Sugar Mountain had their fill of the big, wide world, Mayor Stern was ready. Waiting. Planning. Plotting.

"It's kind of like waiting for salmon to come back up the river to spawn," he once told Matt Skylar.

"Counting the days and weeks before they come back. And they always come back."

The yearly high school reunions were an integral part of his scheme. The streets were festooned with brilliant banners of green and white, the Sugar Mountain High School colors. Mayor Stern's bar offered free drinks and a side order of his famous onion ring loaf to every returning alumni. Mr. Hunt, owner and sole realtor at the Hunt Realty Company, threw a large party for alumni during which he displayed pictures of Sugar Mountain homes which had recently come on the market.

The junior varsity football team endured an exhaustive seminar on the lineup of teams ten, fifteen, and twenty years past. Coach Scandaglia told his men that alumni players would be only too happy to recount moving details of long-ago games, games that would be the subject of a written test on the next Monday, which would determine the team's starting positions.

The elementary school students sang the school songs at the reunion cocktail party on Friday night— the nostalgic smiles and cries of *they're-so-cute!* from the audience were in sharp contrast to the rolled eyes and groans those tunes had once elicited from them when they had been younger and wiser. The local radio station played Sugar Mountain Elementary's school song—*'Tis a Gift to Be Simple, 'Tis a Gift to Be Free*—every quarter hour until even the president of the Chamber of Commerce was ready to scream.

On Mondays after Reunion Weekend, in his office at Village Hall, Mayor Stern would open a succession of old yearbooks, circling the pictures of the ones who would stay. The ones who had traveled the world and figured out you won't find anything you haven't got in your own backyard. The ones who were finding out it takes a village to raise a child and Sugar Mountain was an awfully good village. The ones who had made a little money, lost a little money, and didn't need to chase the dollar to be happy. The ones who wanted to come home.

Every five years a yearbook would be updated. Twenty-year-old yearbooks were the ones he lingered over. Lots of pages with circled pictures. And thirty— well, he had taken the liberty of circling his own picture in bright-red pen, even though he had never left.

The future, that's what he was preserving, the future of Sugar Mountain.

He had long known that the reunion coming nine-and-a-half years after the death on Sugar Mountain was going to be a challenge. Jack would have been in the class coming in for his fifteenth reunion. The next Skylar brother TJ was certain not to attend his reunion, and his absence would only highlight the fact that he had never in the past ten years set foot in his hometown. Mayor Stern worried for Matt, the only Skylar brother who had stayed home, who had filled out a job application at Village Hall the week after his brother's death.

On Thursday morning, as Mayor Stern reviewed the weekend's schedule, he picked up his phone to call Matt. He started to dial and then hung up. What could he say? *I know this is going to be a tough one? Thank you for all the help you've given to me and the village during the years since your brother's death? Sorry TJ doesn't come back? Sorry nobody has a clue where Win fled to? Sorry that you're the one who has to care for your mother, a woman so overcome with grief and rage that she hasn't stepped out of her house since the funeral of her eldest son?*

In the end, Mayor Stern did what he was good at. He picked up the phone again, dialing before he could reconsider, and told Matt in a strictly business way that the fireworks display the fire department had planned for Saturday night was officially approved and would Matt like to stop by the bar tonight for a beer before all the alumni got into town and took the best seats?

Mayor Stern focused on these details because it was easier than tackling the dark, foreboding truth. Sugar Mountain had no future to offer its returning brood. He looked out his office window to the corner of Main Street and Eastman Avenue. The ladies' dress shop still had the going-out-of-business-sale sign in the window, though its doors hadn't been open in two months. The bookstore kitty-corner to Village Hall was offering 10% off each purchase, but it was only a matter of time, with the big superstores taking over. The potholes and the dying elm that should have been cut down grated on Mayor Stern's nerves and he looked away.

One name passed his lips. In uncharacteristic but fully felt anger and sorrow.

"James Burleson," he said.

"What are you doing here?" TJ asked.

Herman tipped his baseball cap at a passing woman.

"I just dropped off the title to my car. Miss Burleson's car."

"And where is she?"

"On her way to get her car."

"Why didn't you take her back to get the car?"

"I wanted to see the sights. You see, me and Berte have never been to Chicago and certainly never to such a beautiful hotel." He gazed admiringly at the faux Grecian columns. "We are even considering going downstairs to Trader Vic's for some of those wicked *mai tais* this evening."

TJ had a sudden inspiration.

"Need a place to stay?"

Herman shook his head, smiling at the notion of a simple car mechanic and his sister taking a room at the finest hotel in Chicago.

"We can't afford this place. We're getting two rooms at the Motel 8 on Congress Parkway."

"No, no," TJ said, leading Herman to the reception desk. He touched the counter bell, and a delicate grace note caught the desk clerk's attention. "Could we have an extra key for my friend Herman and his sister? Oh, and they'll be staying for a few days in my suite. When they check out, send the bill to my New York office."

The desk clerk looked at Herman and then at TJ.

"Certainly, sir," he said and reached into his drawer for a key. "Anything else, sir?"

"Yes, a reservation for two at seven o'clock at Trader Vic's. Put the bill on my tab."

"Very good, sir."

Herman shook his head at TJ's generosity.

"Herman, I've got one last question for you. Where's Paige's little red sports car?"

"*Ja,* I fixed it," he said proudly. "I welded together a part out of materials I had in the shop. I brought it here for her but she said since I loved it so much I could still have it. She'd keep my big yellow one."

"How much do you love her car?"

Herman's eyebrows drew together.

"What do you mean by that, Mr. Skylar?"

"Call me TJ. I want to know what your favorite automobile is."

"No question about that. A BMW Z3, convertible, blue. The James Bond Blue. I've rented *Tomorrow Never Dies* six times just so I could see that vehicle. I pause it and linger."

"Herman, let's go visit a showroom right now. I want to work out a little trade."

TJ thought about Paige all through the eighteen-hour drive, even turned off his pager—which had the most annoying and predictable habit of announcing that the office needed him. He was sure he would find her in Sugar Mountain; and as he drove ever higher and higher through the mountain pass, he thought about where to look first: her parents' house, the high school, even Mayor Stern's bar.

Never once did he think of going where he ended up—at the precipice overlooking the charming, twinkling, unchanging lights of Sugar Mountain Village. He parked Paige's red sports car on the shoulder and climbed. She led him, as surely as if she were still in the car, tricking him to abandon his Wall Street office for a phantom client. His gait was tentative; his hiking boots felt awkward. But the ground was warm and moist and a mountain man never forgets. Soon his steps were sure and strong. He reached the top, looked out over the valley.

This mountain had raised him, nurtured him, guided him to manhood. But this mountain had also been cruel, extracting a terrible price. His brother's death was with him, every day as if it were the day Jack had fallen out of his hands.

He had failed, his brother's fingers slipping from his grip. And all failures, every shortcoming, every weakness sprang from this first tragedy, this first notion that he had no right to confidence, no right to believe in himself.

What could he offer Paige? Love? Marriage? Children?

None of these, a voice inside him cried, for in all these he would fail; surely he would. And he would be responsible for a fall of a different kind.

Better to go, he thought, resolving to turn back. *Go back to New York.* Do what he could do, do what he could succeed at.

And as he turned away from the valley, he felt something at his hand. He glanced over his shoulder. Saw nothing. But still, felt pressure on his fingertips, a squeezing grip . . .

Nothing. He believed in nothing. Nothing outside of what was real, what was in front of his eyes. Nothing.

And yet, he walked back, reluctantly, to the precipice. Looked out over the valley. He felt a chill on his back; the shirt wasn't enough. He was sure that snow clouded his vision. He felt his brother's hand. Tugging downward, fingers clawing, the smell of fear, a rippling of stone and dirt as Jack sought purchase on unforgiving rock.

The touch of his brother's flesh. One touch. And while he thought it pure hokum, was already rationalizing that lack of sleep or too much sleep or not enough vitamins or too many vitamins was creating the conditions for temporary psychological disturbance, he kept his hand out and crouched at the precipice edge. For he had missed his brother, had given up so much of his life in missing his brother, that he was hungry for any piece of Jack—even if it was madness.

He crouched there, feeling the wind at his back, his younger brother's panic. He saw Jack turn his head toward the valley, away from the rock and soil.

"It's so beautiful," he had said.

Again and again, in TJ's mind, he said it still.

But this time, ten years later, Jack said something more.

"Let go, TJ. I'm letting go."

"No, you go, we all go," TJ repeated.

"Not this time, brother."

And then Jack's fingers went limp. TJ couldn't hold his grip. Dead weight. His fingers were so damn slippery and cold.

The feeling was gone.

"Jack!" he yelled. But there was no one to answer him.

You go, we all go.

He had lived up to that motto. He had gone, withdrawing from his family, his village, even from himself, as if he could be like Jack.

But it was Jack who had let go. It wasn't TJ.

TJ opened his clenched hand.

He stood up and turned around. He was alone. All alone. He picked up a clump of soil and threw it over the edge. And after saying goodbye, he got in Paige's car and drove into town.

The mayor's bar was just as he remembered—ash wood planks not quite covered with green paint. Two old-timers, couldn't possibly be the same men he saw ten years ago, sat on an upholstered couch on the porch. The couch was for summer. In winter, there'd be an illuminated plastic nativity scene, complete with shepherds, wise men, Santa, and Frosty the Snowman.

A banner hung over the steps—*Welcome Home*—and the sign was kept up so long during the year that most folks called the mayor's tavern the Welcome Home, though its real name was the Estelle Bar—named for the mayor's late mother.

TJ walked up the steps, a squeal on the fourth step reminding him of past forays to this watering hole.

Once he opened the door, his eyes took a moment to adjust to the darkness, a sharp contrast to the blazing sunlight outside. He blinked as someone called out his name. And then the features of the bar cleared—a brass-railed bar stretched the length of the dining room; ten plank tables were scattered throughout the floor, facing a stage with the mayor's gold trumpet propped against a bar stool. All as he remembered it. Right down to the seven-foot-tall Jethro Tull poster over the fireplace.

"TJ, hey, man, how ya doin'?" Mayor Stern called from the table by the window. Delicate white lines marred an otherwise perfect tan, but his jeans still fit well on a runner's sleek frame. His short hair said *public official,* but every other attribute marked him as *still groovy after all these years.*

TJ's outstretched hand fell limp at his side when he realized the man who sat with the mayor was his brother.

"Matt," he said, feeling stilted and unsure of himself. "How are you?"

Matt stood up. He had grown into a powerful man. With a badge. He extended a hand and both men started to shake and then awkwardly hugged.

"Glad you're home," Matt said softly.

They broke apart and the mayor insisted that he had to run along on some unspecified official business.

"Stay and have a beer," he offered. "And while you're catching up on old times, try my onion loaf. It's complimentary during Reunion Week. And this is your reunion week. Party on!"

"Actually, I'm not staying for the reunion. I'm just looking for another alumni," TJ said. "Paige Burleson."

Mayor Stern's look of surprise at the news that TJ wasn't staying hardened into disapproval.

"Is James's daughter coming in?"

"Yeah, is that a problem?"

"I don't think she's going to find herself particularly welcome here," the mayor said. "A lot of people blame her father."

"For what?" TJ demanded.

The mayor and Matt exchanged a solemn look.

"This town is dying," Matt said quietly. "And Mr. Burleson is regarded by many as the reason."

"What the—"

"I'll let you talk it over with your brother," the mayor said. "Just keep an eye on her. Feelings run pretty deep around here. I can't imagine why she chose to come back here now."

TJ would have asked more, but a young, pert-bodied woman stepped forward to ask Mayor Stern if he wanted to go to the movies with her this afternoon. The mayor pleaded official business, but the woman's disappointment made him reconsider.

"All right," he said. "But I have to be back in time for the reunion cocktail party."

"Absolutely, Mr. Mayor!"

"That man has always been a babe magnet," Matt observed, shaking his head at the couple. "And I can't for the life of me figure out why."

"It's been like that since he got elected. Must be the office, not the man."

A bartender slid a beer mug in front of TJ and refreshed Matt's coffee.

"Welcome back," Matt said awkwardly. "I know it must be hard."

"Yeah, well, can't say I want to be here," TJ admitted. "Nothing personal."

Matt nodded.

Long since the point where it bothered him that his brother had left him behind.

Since it bothered him the way a six-inch knife to his heart would bother him.

Now it was more like a dull ache around his temples when he thought too long about the years going by with a family torn apart.

"So what's going on?" TJ asked. "What's all this talk about Sugar Mountain dying?"

"Things have changed a lot since you've left," Matt said.

TWENTY

"Your father's a mighty unpopular man these days," Paige's mother said quietly.

Paige looked up from the stack of papers on her father's desk. Outside the smoked-glass door, the bank was mournfully lit and its employees talked as they worked as if they were at a funeral.

Which they were, Paige thought as she straightened the papers neatly.

"Ma, this is a lot worse than I can handle," Paige said. "I will give the bank every penny I've saved, my pension fund, and I'll—"

"I'm giving up my retirement money," her mother interrupted. "I called the fund managers and they said that it's possible for schoolteachers to take their pensions in a lump sum. And, of course, we'd sell the house."

"Ma, my point is it's still not going to be enough. I'm sorry. I know you didn't realize how bad it was."

Her mother sniffed into her wrinkled handkerchief.

"Paige, couldn't we sell the bank?"

"No one's going to want it."

"Well, I can't let him end his life here, among people who will think so badly of him."

"They won't blame him. Other people took advantage of him; he didn't know that he was in over his head. I can do my best," Paige said. "But even **then**, I'm not sure I can fix things."

"Your father's not a bad man, you know."

"I know. His only mistake is that he thought Sugar Mountain was a big town. And it's not. It's a little tiny speck on the map; and that's not a bad thing, as long as you don't try to fit a shopping center and six-screen movie complex on the speck."

"If only he hadn't loaned the money to those men who thought they were going to develop the south valley!"

Paige remembered the acres of land, bounded by a wire fence with a posted sign facing the highway. Site of Sugar Mountain Shopping Mall. Grand Opening . . . That was two years past. The earth plowed and flat and barren. The men and the bank's money—long gone.

"That's one of Dad's mistakes," Paige agreed.

"If the bank goes down, a lot of people are going to lose everything," Ma pointed out. "Sugar Mountain will be a ghost town. It's happened to other places 'round here. South Paw. Tyme's Gate. Tumbleweed Junction. They have an abandoned outlet mall in Tumbleweed."

"I know," Paige said, wearily rubbing her temples. "I'll see what I can do. But I'm staying. I'm staying for the long haul."

"No, Paige, you're throwing away your life. Go back to New York."

"I'm coming back home. If I don't, we really will have to turn the bank over to federal regulators. And then, who knows what will happen to our town?"

"Paige, let me ask you a question. When was the last time I told you I went to a wedding?"

It was an unexpected change of subject.

"Pardon me?"

"When was the last time I went to a wedding?"

"Well, let me think. It must have been the Fitzgerald girl, just three weeks ago at Faith Union. You called me to tell me all about it. Why do you ask?"

"How old is she?"

"I used to babysit her. So, let me see. I was in eighth grade when she was . . . okay, that makes her what? , . . . twenty . . . twenty . . . twenty-two, I think."

"And how many women do you know of that are pregnant right now?"

"In Sugar Mountain? Ma, you write to me every time. Three I can think of. The Jackson girl, Lottie Smith, and Peggy Newman. I used to babysit for Peggy, too."

"How old are they?"

"I think the Jackson girl's twenty-two. Lottie's twenty-four, but this is her third child. And Peggy is twenty."

"Exactly."

"I don't understand what this has to do with . . . oh, Ma. You're thinking that I'm too old for marriage."

"When the children a woman used to babysit are getting married, it's time—"

"There's a lot of women who wait until they're in their late twenties, even thirties."

"Yeah, but they wait in places like New York, Chicago, and L.A. In those cities, a woman who is twenty-eight and unmarried is just that—twenty-eight and unmarried. In Sugar Mountain, they practically bolt from their high school graduation to the altar if they're going to stay in town. Twenty-eight and unmarried is a spinster."

"So your point is that I'll never marry if I come back? Heavens, there're lots of wonderful men who'd be happy to have a relationship with me. We could invite them to dinner. Like Harry Thomas. We'd get along great. He's very shy, though. And a little odd."

"Thank you, no. I won't let my daughter date men who don't have the confidence to be bald if nature took away their hair."

"That's not real?"

Her mother looked up at the ceiling.

"Oh, dear. Well, there's Mr. Krause."

"He's married."

"You told me he was divorced."

"Separated," her mother conceded. "And he has six lovely children."

"Six seems like a lot."

"It would be like having an instant family. And there's another problem. He doesn't believe in working women."

"I'll just have to settle for Mayor Stern."

Her mother's mouth opened to a wide O.

"Absolutely not! He's a libertine."

They both laughed.

"Ma, I'm staying," Paige said. "I'm happy to stay." And then she added so her mother wouldn't worry, "I'm glad to be home."

She looked out the picture window. Sugar Mountain was the perfect town to raise a child, to live with a husband, to prosper as a family. It was not a place for a twenty-eight-year-old single woman.

She worked hard at her smile, convincing her mother that she was delighted to be home. Her mother's gratitude was reward enough that she let go of her worries and her disappointments.

The two women walked out into the bank lobby, where Paige's father sat playing cards with the security guard.

"This is a nice place," he told Paige. "Can we come back tomorrow?"

Paige bit back tears and nodded, promising her father that he could come back, knowing that by tomorrow he wouldn't remember he had asked, not any more than he would remember that this was the bank he had built, the one he had raised up by hard work and drive, before the disease of forgetfulness had brought him and his bank down.

"The Knack," TJ said when he entered her bedroom after a barely there knock. "I never knew you had a thing for The Knack."

Paige looked up from the selection of travel brochures on her bed. She did everything in her power not to leap up and give him a hug. He was home!

"The Knack was actually very talented," she said primly.

"Right."

They both laughed at the long-forgotten teen band.

"You're here," Paige said quietly.

"I had a high school reunion to go to," TJ said. "And also a friend I had to apologize to."

"You already apologized."

"Then let me spend the rest of my life repeating myself."

"What about Shawna?"

"If you turn on the evening news, you'll see her at her press conference announcing that she's the new CEO of SunOil Motorcon Corporation."

"The Oil-Me-Up Girl is going to be a CEO? That is worth sitting through the headlines from Washington. But how'd that happen?"

"Long story. Don't get me sidetracked. I want to tell you that I can't be your friend anymore. I'm a man. And I've got one thing on my mind. Loving you. All the time. And I know women are complex creatures. They've got lots of dreams and ambitions, and if loving you means I have to work every minute of my life making those dreams come true, baby, I will."

She started to cry, just a little teariness around the edges. Thinking about all he couldn't give up. All she couldn't have.

"Marry me, Paige, and I promise I'll make every one of your dreams come true."

Now the tears were coming in earnest as she did what she knew she had to do.

"No," she said.

"No?" he asked. Momentarily puzzled, because so very seldom in his life had he heard a woman say *no* to him. And certainly he wouldn't have expected a marriage proposal to be met this way.

"No," Paige said. "We want different things in life. You want Manhattan. I want the mountains. You want excitement and tension every day, and I want to feel some peace. I won't have a marriage that's a sacrifice for you and I can't leave. . . ."

He touched his index finger to her lips.

"I want what you want," he said. "I just didn't know it. I had forgotten how much I love Sugar Mountain. I had forgotten how much I loved you. I trained myself to be someone I wasn't—because, after Jack's accident, I felt I had failed at being . . . at being myself."

"You were not a failure," Paige whispered. "You held on to Jack's hand as long as you could."

"I know that now," TJ said. "And I know now that Jack let go. He knew we were both going to go down together if he didn't."

"Oh, my God," Paige said, horrified.

"No, no, it's a good thing he did," TJ said. "He made the decision to save my life. Do you know what the last words he said were?"

She shook her head.

"That it was beautiful. Sugar Mountain. And he was right."

He ran his fingers through her hair, wiped away a tear that sparkled on her cheek.

"I didn't want to come back, to face my failings. But you dragged me here, kidnapped me, coaxed me, set me right when I detoured, tricked me in every way possible. And now that I'm here, I know the most important part of myself that I forgot."

"What was that?"

"That I agreed with him. Now, tell me, woman, will you marry me?"

"Yes, but—"

"Yes, but what?"

* * *

They drove out to the Skylar house in Paige's sports car. On the way, TJ told her about taking Herman and Berte to the Field's BMW dealership in Chicago.

"He picked out the same model and color as the one Pierce Brosnan drove in *Tomorrow Never Dies.* Oh, my God, would you look at that?"

The immaculately groomed lawn of the Skylar home was exactly as it had been ten years before. The gravel in the driveway was raked so that it looked like the icing on a delicious cake. Hostas and late-blooming daffodils burst towards pathways and steps. Trumpet vines grew up and around the first-floor windows. An indigo clematis wound lazily around the banister to the front porch.

"Matt must take care of the landscaping," TJ opined.

"Mayor Stern says she gets her weekly groceries delivered by Lakeside Foods," Paige said. "The driver is instructed to leave the bags by the back door. He's never actually seen her, although she does leave out an envelope with a twenty-dollar tip at Christmas. She does everything else by mail. The only person she lets in the house is Matt."

"Did he stay because of her?"

"You'd have to ask him," Paige said, putting the emergency brake on. "But he could have gone anywhere."

"And it was from the day of the funeral."

"From the moment she came home."

"I never talked to her."

"I know."

"She told me she thought I didn't do as much as I could. That I was the one who killed him by not hanging on . . ."

"I know."

"Do I have to do this?"

"Yes," she replied firmly.

They walked up the path to the front porch, careful to step over the rotted wood. TJ rang the doorbell.

"Ma! Ma! Open up."

Nothing.

"If I told you that she's not home, you wouldn't believe me, would you?" TJ asked.

"No, I wouldn't," Paige said, ringing the doorbell again.

They waited. He felt tension coiling up his spine.

"Okay, I'm outta here."

"TJ, no."

A shadow passed along the lace curtain falling on the door window. The door opened ever so slightly.

"Ma," TJ said.

A deep breath in shadow and then the door was pulled back to reveal a small, hunched woman. For a second, TJ wondered how his dead grandmother could be here, alive, wearing a dress he remembered from his childhood, dirty now, ripped in a few places . . . and then, shocked, he realized this woman, this broken woman, was his mother. Staring at him with one arm thrown up against her face to shield her from sunlight.

"You brought him back," she said in wonder.

"Yes, Mrs. Skylar, I did."

"My son," she said, reaching to him. She wanted

him to embrace her. And TJ couldn't; he just couldn't. He could feel sorry for her. Send her money. Hire a professional to get her out of the house. He could even talk to her. Visit awhile. But to open up to her. To love her, feel for her, after all these years of knowing that she held him responsible . . .

He bolted down the steps and charged halfway across the front lawn.

Then he heard Paige's voice.

"TJ," she pleaded.

He stopped.

"TJ," she repeated.

And what could he do? He loved her. Loved her more than himself. He turned around. Walked slowly up the steps. Into his mother's embrace. Paige slipped her hand into his. And they both felt Mrs. Skylar's quivering sobs.

"Ma, I did everything I knew how to do," he said. "Please . . ."

She pulled away from him.

"No, please listen. I lost one son and my anger at the fates infected everything—even my love for you. I held you responsible, thought you were to blame; but you did everything you could. You tried your hardest."

"Yeah, I did."

"Then, please, TJ, do something harder. Forgive me."

What could he do? What could he say? Of course, of course, but the words of forgiveness—would they be real? He opened his mouth, started to speak, and then felt Paige's touch. Her hand at his back. The warmth of her love in that touch.

"Ma, of course, I forgive you," he said.

And the words were true. Mrs. Skylar had her son back.

The mayor called the Burleson home at seven that evening.

"Mrs. Burleson, I'm returning your call," he said briskly.

"Oh, yes, I wanted to tell you—TJ Skylar is back. He's upstairs with Paige. They're playing her old records. Such a sweet thing to do, don't you agree?"

"Sure. Tell him that his class reunion party is at the elementary school gym. Same as Paige's."

"Okay. And I have a message for you. The reason why I called. Paige will be our new bank president. I think that would be a very good thing for Sugar Mountain."

There was a long pause.

"That's great news. Tell the new president that I'd like to have lunch next week with her and the Chamber of Commerce to discuss community development. We'll have a lot of work to do, but I'm confident she'll come through."

"I'm sorry about my husband. He hasn't been well."

"When your daughter takes over, it won't matter what happened in the past."

After she hung up, Mrs. Burleson walked upstairs and knocked on her daughter's door. Getting no answer, perhaps because the Luther Vandross music was so loud, she tried the door knob. The door was locked—and Mrs. Burleson remembered that in a fit of teenaged pique, Paige had put a lock on the door. What possible use could she have for one now?

She knocked again, louder this time, and got no answer.

"It's like having her turn fifteen again." Mrs. Burleson sighed, giving up. She got halfway down the steps when she heard the door open. But it closed again quicker than she could turn around. A note had been taped to the door. Mrs. Burleson approached and smiled as she read it. "Engaged Couple. Keep Out!"

"I told her if she moved back home, she'd have a tough time fending off the suitors!"

TJ paused midkiss, lifting his head from the sweet flesh of her shoulder.

"I heard her knock again," he said.

"You did not. That was the music."

"I did, too. Your mother, she was at the door."

"She's looking at the note. The door's locked."

"That doesn't mean she didn't knock."

He started to rise, but she pulled him to her with her thighs.

"Paige, I feel like a teenager again," he said. "We shouldn't be . . ."

She touched him lightly with her fingertips, just below the hipbone where the flesh was taut and hard.

"When you touch me like that—" He moaned, his eyes turning a liquid-chocolate color. "Paige, tell me again; will you marry me?"

His last words were lost in his climax. She waited until his breath stilled.

"Are you going to ask me that every time we make love?"

He ground his hips against her.

"Only if I can get the answer I want. And you know what I want."

And it was then, just then, that she replied, the soft breath of the word pressed against his chest as the first concentric waves shuddered through her body.

"Yes, darling, yes," she sighed. "I'll marry you."

EPILOGUE

A wedding was as good as a reunion, Mayor Stern thought as he stood with the guests on the steps of Faith Union. Weddings brought people together, made them think about the future, made them think about settling down. And what finer place to build one's nest than the little village in the valley of the Sugar Mountain peaks?

The bridesmaids emerged from the church—one each on the arms of the young Police and Fire Chief Matt Skylar. Kate and Zoe were as pretty as could be in dresses the pale blue of the sky at sunset. And then Teddy sauntered out with the ring pillow. Mayor Stern didn't know much about the boy, just that he was the son of one—no, all three—of the women. Matt tousled the boy's hair.

The mayor didn't see the Skylar matriarch, but then he had been seated near the back of the church, and during the reception in the church basement, he had been so busy mingling that he hadn't thought of her. Now he stood far from the center of the joyous crowd; so, perhaps he had simply missed the chance to say hello to the older Mrs. Skylar. As for her youngest son, Winfield, Mayor Stern hoped that one day the boy would return—although he had to remind himself that the youngest Skylar boy would be a man.

The crowd hurrahed as the newlyweds emerged. TJ was tall and confident. He accepted congratulations from the auto mechanic from Pennsylvania who had arrived at the nuptials with a car that made Mayor Stern somewhat envious. The mayor smiled when he caught sight of the newly appointed president of the Sugar Mountain Community Bank. Her gown was a fluffy white confection of tulle and silk. She kissed both Cruikshank sisters and Krysha the baker burst into tears.

Mayor Stern wondered if it were selfish to be glad that the couple was going to have only a one-day honeymoon before returning to the bank. There was a lot of work to do to get the town's economy back on track, and Mayor Stern was anxious to begin.

The bride held up her hand to shield herself from the torrent of rice. TJ hustled her to the car, shaking hands all along the way, making Mayor Stern for the first time consider that there was a citizen of this town who could be trained to take his place in the distant future when he would consider retirement.

Just before she got in the car, Paige threw her bouquet of calla lillies back to the crowd.

Folks got a hearty chuckle when Matt Skylar ended up with the flowers.

Even Mayor Stern couldn't resist a smile. Just two weeks ago at the Martins' party Kate and Matt had announced that they were married—and then that they weren't. And now Kate was giving Matt a kiss. It was enough to make a small-town mayor's head spin.

The limousine sped off, a dozen empty cans and two cowboy boots tied to its back grille. The mayor sighed, satisfied. Ah, yes, the mood in Sugar Mountain was good, a pleasant feeling having settled on the mountains as surely as snow touched the peaks and valleys.

Mayor Stern shook a few folks' hands, made small talk with a couple of people, got a finger-wagging from a Cruikshank sister, and winked at a few women—all as was his habit. Then he sauntered over to his tavern where he intended to while away a few hours playing the trumpet and thinking about how beautiful this Sugar Mountain was.

Turn the page for a preview of
THE MEN OF SUGAR MOUNTAIN:
TWO HEARTS

Coming from Bouquet in June!

It really wasn't so bad, Kate thought. The cold wasn't bothering her anymore. Her high-heeled pumps didn't hurt. In fact, she couldn't really feel her toes anymore. Her fear was gone, fear that had been so close and so real it was as if it were sitting on the trunk of the Corvette waiting to remind her that everything about her was a failure.

Even her feet seemed to be warming up a little, if that were possible.

A tiny voice in her head said, "Careful. Hypothermia does that to a person, makes them lose their judgment and do something stupid."

"But I didn't lose my judgment out here," Kate said aloud. Her words competed and lost with the wind. "And all the stupid things I've already done were long before I got out here."

She laughed at her joke and stood knee-deep in beautiful snow, watching for the lights. They seemed to be coming from two different directions now. Confusing her. She wondered if she had turned—because if she had, she shouldn't go forward. Toward the farmhouse. She should go this way. Toward the car. No. That way.

Where was she? Oh, yes, lost her judgment. Bad judgment. Stupid. In men, yes. Absolutely the worst.

Only two men in her life, ever, and she had to pick Lawrence . . . and Matt Skylar.

Not that it was so bad picking Lawrence Vander-Norton III. He was, after all, her husband. And not that he was a bad man. Not like Matt at all. Oh, no, he was a one-eighty on Matt. Lawrence was kind, well-mannered, cultivated, and handsome in a delicate, aristocratic way. He was a respected Boston investment banker who dabbled in academic subjects. He didn't fall asleep at operas. Understood ballet. And was as unwavering in his morality as she would like to be in hers.

And he had given her the one thing she had always craved from a man—respect. Something her mother never had. Something she never would have had if she had stayed in Sugar Mountain.

But love?

Did he love her?

How could he love her and want a divorce? How could a man who was a man give up his wife so easily? What kind of woman was she that she deserved to be cast aside? Did her husband love her? Did she love him?

"Hypothermia setting in," she said, and determined to move on.

She lifted her foot up and put it down in virgin snow. Down, down. Such beautiful snow. And when she lay down to worship its beauty, some little part of her knew that this was folly. So beautiful, so soft, like velvet really . . .

And just as she felt the tender, loving snow envelop her, she was scooped up into rough wool and a man's hard, unforgiving arms.

"Let go of me!" she protested, hitting him as hard as she could. It was too dark to see who he was, but there was something unsettlingly familiar about his scent, even in the clear, freshly iced air. She caught him on the shoulder and she was pleased with the satisfying yowl and how he let go, even if only for a moment. The snow was so beautiful and she was so tired. "I was just touching the snow."

"Dammit, Kate, you're freezing out here!"

That voice! She knew who he was; and if he were some apparition created by hypothermia, there was still something very satisfying about what she did next.

She hit him. Once and then again, this time belting him in the kidneys. His own fault—he had thrown her like a sack of potatoes over his shoulder. The indignity of it all! She kicked and thought she got purchase on his hipbone. He stumbled, cursed her, and righted himself. She squirmed around, ripping off his flap-eared hat.

A curse died on his lips. A splash of headlight focused on his cheeks—red with little wind-tear icicles running down his face to his jaw. His hair was shorter than he'd kept it in high school. Twin lines of worry between his eyebrows and lines of mirth around his mouth confirmed he was no creation of her memory, stilled at eighteen years of age.

"Damn it, Kate, don't hit me again," he shouted against the wind. "You're acting nuts. Just settle . . . oh, man, that hurt bad!"

She had used a satisfying right hook, but it hadn't come without cost. With one hand he gripped both her wrists, and with the other he hoisted her legs around his waist so that even her best kicks netted little result.

"I just want to lie down," she screamed. "For just one minute! Then I'll go wherever it is you . . ."

He wasn't listening. He climbed through the snow-drifts toward one set of lights; she couldn't tell whether toward her Corvette or toward the farmhouse she once thought she was nearing. Her face was buried in the collar of his barn jacket, but there was a sliver of warm, exposed flesh. She moved her face so that she could smell its scent.

And all the fight went out of her. There was still confusion, to be sure. But she didn't struggle. She let herself go limp. Let him carry her, strong and purposeful as he was.

"Matt," she said into his flesh. "You can let go of my hands."

He grunted. Pulling one of his legs out of the snow and putting it back in just a few feet away. Rough going. *Never going to make it,* she thought. *It would be so beautiful just to lie down in the snow.*

"Matt, I promise I'm not going to hit you again. It must have been the cold. And I haven't eaten in awhile. I've been driving for nearly three days straight, only got a few hours sleep back in Iowa. Please, please."

The please must have worked.

He put her down on the snow, but only just long enough to wrap a blanket around her and pick her up again. It was then that she was sure that she was suffering from hypothermic dementia, that temporary insanity people get from exposure.

Hypothermic dementia is a mercy of nature, one

that allows the frozen doomed to believe that they are warm and comforted, enjoying a full stomach and no pain. Even perhaps believing that the snow is a thing of beauty not to be feared. No struggle, no anguish, no terror.

She was sure that she suffered from this condition, though there was no sense of comfort or sleepiness. Just an agitation that made her flail and push and shove against him.

No comfort for the weary and cold; yet what moved her had to be dementia because the next words out of her mouth were completely out of character.

"Matt," she said, pushing her face out from the warmth of his flesh and of the blanket. "Matt. Please. Kiss. Me."

BOOK YOUR PLACE ON OUR WEBSITE AND MAKE THE READING CONNECTION!

We've created a customized website just for our very special readers, where you can get the inside scoop on everything that's going on with Zebra, Pinnacle and Kensington books.

When you come online, you'll have the exciting opportunity to:

- View covers of upcoming books

- Read sample chapters

- Learn about our future publishing schedule (listed by publication month *and author*)

- Find out when your favorite authors will be visiting a city near you

- Search for and order backlist books from our online catalog

- Check out author bios and background information

- Send e-mail to your favorite authors

- Meet the Kensington staff online

- Join us in weekly chats with authors, readers and other guests

- Get writing guidelines

- AND MUCH MORE!

**Visit our website at
http://www.zebrabooks.com**

Put a Little Romance in Your Life With
Fern Michaels